Captain Heart

By

GEORGE ADATSI

Editor: Brad Green | brad@hasmarkpublishing.com
Cover Artist: Anne Karklins | anne@hasmarkpublishing.com
Layout Design: Amit Dey | amit@hasmarkpublishing.com

ISBN 13: 978-1-989756-76-8
ISBN 10: 198975676X

Dedication

Wow! Finally, I'm actually doing this. I'm getting some of my inner voices out on paper and to the public. As John Lennon said, "I am he as you are he as you are me and we are all together." I want to dedicate this book to everyone who kept going in the search for their desired reality, fueled by their dreams and expectations; I know how deeply you feel, how much you want, and how well you laugh and smile when you make it through. The most beautiful results are the smile, the laughter, the moment of love when time stops and we get younger, lighter, more connected with our soul, every time we visit that place called *Joy*!

I want to dedicate this book to all those who never quit, who listened to that little voice inside that gave you an idea and you fell for it. You took it, picked it up, and shaped it into the bright and shining diamond it has become! *Becoming*: that's the main goal of this book. To help readers all over the world become whatever they desire. You will become something or someone. Take the chance while you actually have it and sculpt yourself into what you want to become. The time will be there, and so will the laws of physics. The love and passion, light and darkness, sun and rain, happiness and joy—they will be there. The only ingredient you can't forget to include is your vision, your idea, your input! You are the missing ingredient in the magical formula that makes your dreams come true.

Thank you for your gift.

George Adatsi

Contents

Acknowledgments

I'd like to thank a few people for all their contributions, either intentional or unintentional, who added to the content of this book. As this book it centered on my life—my experience on earth this time around—it's inevitable that I mention a few, as I couldn't have done it without them.

To my grandmother, for receiving me in her home during my post-heart attack period and my early recovery. For the invaluable conversations and your support of my desire to become fully free and alive—a heart-felt thank you.

To my uncle and sponsor, Mr. F, for his patience and eternal support. A Royal thank you.

To my parents! Regardless of their plans, I was born at a time and in the environment that I consciously chose, giving them no choice but to raise me! I'm forever grateful. I couldn't have chosen a better place and better companions to develop with. Thank you.

To my mentors, coaches, and teachers who believed in me and the beauty of my dreams, and who saw the potential that I believed I had and pushed me through to becoming someone they can be proud of.

I'd like to thank you for reading this book. This is for you. I hope you enjoy it and get something extraordinary out of it.

Lastly, I'd like to thank myself—my inner voice, the source of my ideas and desires to stand true to my beliefs—for chasing my ideas and dreams. For ignoring the norm and continuing to follow through, connecting to our origins and potential abilities.

Have fun reading!

Preface

The powerful clarity of thought.

W here am I? I am sitting on the deck of a 54-meter sailing yacht anchored in the beautiful bay of Tavolara, a small island on the east coast of Sardinia. My girlfriend and I have been methodically alternating between bathing in the sun and swimming fully naked in the warm waters of the Mediterranean. With its bold, blue, crystal-clear water, the Tyrrhenian sea is a sought-after spot for the rich and famous. Large yachts packed with successful musicians, artists, businessmen, models and designers, along with Arab and Russian oligarchs—your typical billionaires of the world. An exquisite meeting point for holidays, late lunches, fantastic parties, and great business deals on the newest and most exclusive yachts to sail these shores. It's an amazing space and a fantastic time to be alive and kicking in this far distant corner of the universe that we call Earth.

nice

And here I am, next to the rich and famous, the royals, and the successful ones, sharing this experience with my German partner; the beautiful and elegant Spanish language teacher who I met while sailing the West Indies in Antigua two years earlier. She had been visiting another yacht that I was sailing on—a 60-meter modern classic schooner—and we locked eyes immediately. We had both sailed across the Atlantic Ocean on different yachts in search of adventure and excitement, far from the regulated and pressurized European rules. We immediately hit it off, falling for each other within seconds. The attraction was instantaneous, not only due to the picturesque backdrop of a stylish yacht at the historical marina at Nelson's Dockyard, but also due to the fact that I could understand her perfectly as we chatted fluently in Spanish. She was very impressed, and she later admitted this factor had sealed the deal!

Here we were after sailing together for some time, lounging on a $20 million yacht. What had revealed itself to be a true gift from the universe was delivered to us by the captain and his crew to enjoy during a long farewell weekend. Having sailed the world on a variety of yachts, we had been working on this vessel over the summer and would soon be leaving her. It had been our shared home, but now we were ready to move on to a new journey and adventure. It was one of the best weekends of my life! I lived every moment on this yacht as if it were my own. Imagining the feeling of owning it, allowing the enjoyment to sink in, taking the opportunity to ingrain on me the person I wanted to become—a multimillionaire who owns a yacht! I could feel my life being written on the ether of our existence. We loved it so much; sleeping under the starry sky, swimming in the warm ocean, loving each other, and absorbing the abundance and plenitude we had always desired for ourselves. We took it all in, accepting every moment, living it as a reward from the universe! We were delighted with this fantastic moment in time—a dream come true in a paradisiac island on a fabulous yacht. We felt that we must have done something right to have had this come our way. (I won't say the name of the yacht in case its owner reads this book one day. And if one day he finds out, a big thank you from us, from the heart!)

Over the previous three days we had sailed from Turkey to the east coast of Italy, averaging a speed of 14 knots. This is not fast compared to a car or a plane, but pretty awesome for a 350-ton yacht. Pushing, trimming, sending, and sailing it like we stole her between dark clouds, pouring rain, and 30-knot gusts. Day and night, she did what she was made for. We'd been carried by the *meltemi*, the northerly winds traditionally formed between the high pressures of the Greek mainland and the low pressure coming out of Turkey. The meltemi winds usually blow nonstop for three to seven days, much to the delight of most sailors in the area, and we were on it!

Another amazing week of stretching her legs and finding the abilities of this beautiful Italian yacht that was designed by a well-known naval architect. We took her from Bodrum, where we stopped after a Greek Island cruise, and said goodbye to land all the way to the horizon line. My job was to monitor the yacht's performance: watching the rig and sails, checking the weather for winds and currents, and manning the navigational charts, all of which came second nature to me as part of my career at sea. I was employed as a first officer on board, something I'd been chasing for a long time. I heard about the position months before and decided to chase it, as the yacht was going to the Pacific Ocean and would cruise Asia for two years. I didn't get the position immediately, but I did eventually. I met the yacht and her crew at the same yard where we docked for repairs in La Spezia, Italy, and within two weeks, I was in. It finally came to fruition, it happened, and I couldn't have been happier to be part of the team on such a remarkable piece of art. I had always subscribed to the notion that when I want something, I will get it! I wish for it, focus on it, desire it, then I go get it.

It wasn't all fun and games on that beast of a ship. Shortly after our inaugural trip (perhaps three days into our journey), I was struck in the head by a heavy deck hatch. It broke my nose and my face and left me with seven other fractures in the front of my skull. I had to be airlifted off the boat and evacuated to the nearest hospital which was nowhere close to our position in the middle of the ocean. This was an eventful couple of days that I didn't see coming!

This episode happened as we motored down the Italian west coast on a typically calm summer day. The yacht chef showed up on the aft deck complaining about a "banging" noise above his head that was bothering him while he cooked. Note this: if there's anyone you want to keep happy on a boat, it's the cook. And in this case, he was a remarkable chef! I immediately and instinctively volunteered to help him identify the source of this noise and tackle it to ensure he could cook in peace. It makes a difference, trust me; he prepares three meals a day, far from land—they better be good!

It all happened quickly. I went to search for the source of the consistent "banging" sound that was annoying the chef so terribly, only to find a loose aluminum diving bottle rolling sideways, just above his galley deck head. I was laying horizontally on top of a large stainless-steel winch, stretching my arms trying to reach the bottle. As I grabbed and secured it, a large wave caused by a passing ship hit us, causing us to roll. As the boat abruptly moved sideways, the momentum caused the hatch in front of me to violently swing closed. It didn't close all the way, as my face broke its speedy path, serving as a cushion to those heavy "banging" sounds that had been bothering the chef. *Bam! Ouch! Crack! Crash!* Blood everywhere! My face exploded, leaving me in excruciating pain. I rolled under the hatch trying to get up, but I couldn't stand for long as my blood pressure dropped, and I became weak. I kneeled as someone approached to help me stand and walk to the cockpit.

Since rescue service was not available for this type of vessel, we had to sail for another five hours until we got closer land. I finally went ashore in Lipari, a small island in the Ionian Archipelago with a small medical center that could receive me temporarily. They would transport me to a hospital on the mainland, but to get there I'd still need to take a boat ride followed by an ambulance. As it was four o'clock in the morning and nothing could be done until sunrise, they got me a room with a bed where I could wait for a few hours with my girlfriend by my side until she had to leave with the yacht. Thankfully, they accepted my request for painkillers when they saw my injuries. I took overly large swigs of a chemical relaxant to help me sleep while waiting for the first boat out. I vaguely remember being on a bumpy speedboat for a thirty-minute ride to the mainland.

The university hospital in Medina, Sicily, was the closest medical facility that could treat me, so we made our way there. I remember arriving and quickly becoming skeptical due to the dilapidated state of the facility. However, as I was in a lot of pain, I allowed it to happen, trusting the process and realizing this was my only option. The hospital was an old beat-up building straight out of a WWII movie with its traditional beige and brown Italian colors, old doors, and bent metal structures. By the entry door a number of young medical students waited for me. They seemed far too eager to help, wanting to open my face and skull to insert all sorts of tools in an attempt to fix it. They looked like children with new toys, and I was their case study whereby they could explore all types of different medical procedures. It was scary.

One side of my face needed immediate surgery, which happened within two hours of my arrival. The next day, the other side of my face needed surgery as well. Later on, they were deciding about which eye to operate on based on their review of what was clearly an upside-down x-ray. They told me, "We need to operate on your left eye," to which I replied that yesterday the other doctor said that only my right eye needed work. This is when he looks at the scan, flips it right-side up, and replies, "Ah! You're right, we need to operate on the right eye!" That was the moment I realized I needed to find a better hospital! It was so disorganized that I asked to be transferred. You could see that they were unsure of what to do as they turned that x-ray up, down, and sideways, looking for any indication of what could be wrong with me. It was shockingly funny, but I told them, "Please stop. Nobody touches me! I'm leaving."

They tried to stop me, insisting that all would be fine and that everything would be okay. But in the end, after signing a responsibility waiver, they allowed me to leave as they knew I wouldn't stay either way. I was beaten, in pain, and bleeding, my face was bruised and swollen. I wouldn't stop until I was in an airplane on the way to a safer alternative to this crazy little hospital. It was (painfully) hilarious!

The staff assured me that an ambulance would pick me up and take me to the airport. The funny thing is, I thought I was going to die in the ambulance. In a very Italian way, after two hours and still no sign of my transportation, they kept telling me, "It's coming, it's coming." The ambulance finally arrived much later than expected, but that didn't surprise me at all. As we were now late for my flight, the driver decided to floor it. We were going so fast; I thought a racing driver was behind the wheel. Surely only a professional would drive this fast, speeding and cutting corners like there was no tomorrow. We flew through those winding roads, and I've lived in Italy long enough to know the driver was proud of his work. Italians want you to know how fast they can drive!

All the while, the driver was shouting in Italian. I could only understand a few of the words coming from the front seat. I was strapped onto a bed, sloshing around and banging into things as we nearly crashed on a number of occasions. At some point, something fell on my head and they allowed me to take a normal upright seat. Perhaps you've never driven in Italy, but they drive fast and recklessly. It must be either the strong coffee or the massive amounts of it they consume. It is one of my favorite countries in the entire world, but one should be careful on the roads.

Luckily, we made it to the airport in time. We had a laugh, they apologized, and I ran out of the ambulance. I was now set to fly on a private jet for the first time in my life, which I was excited about. I had dreamed about this many times (I guess I never specified in my dreams how I hoped it would happen)! The reason for the private jet was, due to air bubbles behind my eyeballs, I couldn't climb to over twenty-five or thirty thousand feet. Flying higher would cause those air bubbles to explode and that would be unpleasant for all—but especially for me! It was a fantastic flight, with leather seats, varnish, and all the amenities one would expect. It had a German crew that fed me delicious sandwiches and drugged me up so I could fly *tranquillo,* with no pain (and probably to avoid my disturbing them mid-flight). Aside from my ghastly face, it was one of the best flights of my life. The crew and I laughed almost the entire time, chatting about lifestyles and world perspectives.

Meanwhile, the owners of the yacht I was sailing on secured a replacement for my position so they could continue their cruise without delays. I eventually made it home where I was very well received and taken care of, without the need for any more surgeries! It took about eight weeks or so for me to heal and be ready to sail again. I made a full recovery and eventually put my two feet back on that beautiful yacht for a long Turkish trip. However, that's when I got the news that the yacht's captain had decided to keep my stand-in instead of me. They had become good friends and built a team while I was away. So, that was that. Fair enough. When bonds are created between team members, they should be respected, valued, and maintained.

I was shocked for a while, but I quickly applied the theory that everything works out in a perfect way. Deep inside, I trusted that the universe had my back. When one door closes, two windows open. I had faith that something great would come my way. I was surprised, but knew it was for the greater good. I accepted it, looking forward to the next chapter.

As a parting gift, my girlfriend and I got the yacht for a weekend on our own in Sardinia. I didn't mind being fired anymore. I was actually feeling great, happy, and grateful. So, there we were, living the dream in the heat of September on a 180-foot yacht with every imaginable amenity at our fingertips! I felt like I owned that yacht! I was living the part, and it seemed as if all my previous visualization exercises were now paying off. I was truly happy. My circumstances changed from being upset about losing the position to enjoying life and dreaming about what could be a new reality!

I got a new job offer just two days later, and this time it was to go sailing on the latest 60-meter sloop launched in Italy. The project was a cruiser with a racing pedigree, a state-of-the-art *give us all you got* mean machine that surpassed all my expectations. It was a dream yacht; a powerful racing beast with a piano in the salon. I had always wished for that—sailing and playing the piano. This was a perfect movie I could only dream of. The best part is, it just landed on my lap. The yacht would be in Sardinia in a few days to attend a superyacht regatta and would take me on board after the races. In the meantime, we got a hotel for a few days on the island. Little did I know, we'd be invited to race on another stupendous superyacht for the entire week of racing! What a fantastic week. Not only did we stay in the best hotel on the island, but everything was covered for the week. It was nonstop fantastic fun with so many interesting people who became good friends. We sailed every day and won almost every race, which meant champagne and fine dining. We all had a great time. Life is good if we let it be!

My confidence returned, and I again felt that the universe was taking care of me. It took only two days to manifest a new solution, and an incredible one at that, which was probably the result of giving it all I had on the previous project. I must have been doing things the right way. The confusion disappeared and everything felt perfect again. I had a great package, good money coming in, and cruising with the best people in the business. I couldn't be happier, as I felt I was aligned with the universe. I felt fulfilled with an abundance of energy and gratitude, the cosmic reward for my intentions and attitude. I was winning—not *against* anyone, but I was winning with myself. After all, dreams do come true. I was over the moon and ready to take over the oceans.

These were times to celebrate. They were only small steps to many, but they were huge victories for me. I was getting used to winning; I was savoring it and loving each of my successes. But my journey didn't begin like this. Rather, it was a much different start. As far back to my teenage years, I had difficulty fitting in with the cool kids. I wasn't an athlete, and I didn't hang with the smartest cookies. I didn't fit into any of the usual groups. That's how I ended up with the outcasts and the "rock 'n' rollers." As we shared feelings of separateness, loss, and confusion, it quickly led to years of drug abuse and all the guilt that comes along with it.

I didn't know what to do. School was boring, and regardless of whether it was true or not, I felt rejected by the divorce of my parents and their consequent separation. Years later, I found they had their own reasons, and that's okay! But then again, that's the story of every family I know! We all have our teenage issues with parents, brothers, and sisters, and the main point I took away from it was to abandon those issues as soon as possible. We have to let go of any mental system that keeps us in guilt or resentment. Life is beautiful, starting *now*—and that's it! No need for any other explanations or reasons.

At the time, those feelings of rejection became my best awareness, and with the help of psychedelics, I searched for the meaning of life—a quest to expand my consciousness and open the doors of perception. Drugs became my pillars: my best friends, my girlfriends, my lovers, and mistresses. They were always there for me, calling me, luring me into the 60s message of peace and love, nature, understanding, and freedom of expression. I mostly used them in a deep study of the soul, the mind, and our coexistence, experimenting continuously while searching for answers in the ether, in nature, in myself, and in the cosmos. Connecting to higher grounds was pleasing and satisfying! I wanted to know more of the non-visible information that exists in the clouds, and in the air. I had a strong pull toward the stars and what connects them to us, and somehow, this subject had a bigger influence on me than other people's opinions.

However, my endless appetite for drugs eventually led to feelings of alienation, isolation, despair, and emptiness. At some point, I saw no more light. No more wisdom or brightness in the stars. The full swing of addiction had taken over, and I lost all control. My family didn't want me around, and understandably so because of my potential influence on the younger generation.

That should have been a sign. I was in trouble with the law and couldn't stay straight. I had no money or home to live in. Sleeping mostly in my car or in the forest, I would stay anywhere I could, trying to hide and disappear. I was in a miserable state and I had lost everything. Sick, exhausted, and with no escape, I couldn't face anyone. But I finally had to face the truth that was staring straight at me—I had hit rock bottom, and I knew it. I was twenty-four years old.

I quickly realized this wasn't the life I wanted for myself. It wasn't what I had in mind when I began chasing the free world of possibility. I knew I could do better without drugs, but I had to do more than just *dream* of a better life. It was all up to me. I was in charge—no one else. I knew that I could do and be more. Since I was a young boy, I felt that I would be successful. I sensed that I could find a better life and realized I had just chosen the wrong methods and the wrong approach that led me to a tight, dark alley. I could claim a fantastic future. I just needed to have the right thoughts.

Long before this, maybe 12 years earlier, during my early teen years, in order to avoid a long commute, my father got an apartment in the city center for two years where we'd stay during the week for school days. On weekends, we'd return to our base as a family, a countryside house with lots of animals, cats, dogs, and visiting horses and sheep. We were very lucky, and I'm forever grateful for those days, having such a blessed growth and education with a lot of free time and free space to wander. I've always been a tree hugger, and it was normal for me to walk barefoot through woods and puddles. I'd take long walks through the valley and usually stop by a freshwater stream in a hidden part of the forest; such a peaceful place with a special mix of colors, trees, plants, and animals. I was at home in the forest and admired how life was so perfectly organized and easy flowing on those few square meters of land. Near the constant stream of water, plants, ants, bugs, and worms, I lived a peaceful life.

The water ran free and so did everything else around it. And it was beautiful! A variety of interesting vegetation and organic life interlocked, living in effortless harmony, as if they've known each other all of time. Spiders calmly rested on their webs, waiting for their prey. Lizards fed on the spiders along with some flies while little frogs jumped around doing whatever frogs do. A harmonious perfection was hidden behind the bushes, a sampling of a distant world. Who did this? Who built it? Who designed it this way, and why? What for purpose? How did life find its way so clearly and easily from the cosmos to earth, and from earth back into the skies? From where did this perfect harmony originate? Who told the plants how to grow and the spiders how to construct their webs? How did they know how to reach their maximum expression so effortlessly? I was in awe. Pure love energy—just being! Letting it be!

I'd sit amongst nature for hours, admiring this fantastic scene which so resembled a set from a movie. The ecosystem worked like a small city, existing on ten square meters and clearly independent. The beautiful thing was, this small, peaceful, and exemplar slice of a larger forest was perfectly integrated into the blue sphere that is our planet.

I could see the perfection in this environment and sense a natural source of life, an intelligent and secure source, as long as humans wouldn't interfere with it. I'd lose track of time with nature, reading shapes and plant forms, understanding the trees, the bugs, and their movements. The relaxing sound of the stream in the background was hypnotizing. It made me feel as if a show was going on, or an orchestra was playing behind me. Everything flowed perfectly, and mankind had no reason to touch it. We could use it, but not break it. Nature worked well before we arrived. I loved being there in that place; it was so peaceful, respectful and fair!

While growing up in the countryside, another activity that I enjoyed was going out at night and lying on the ground to stare at the starry sky. This was probably my best source of inspiration, the deep night sky. All of those random lights flashing and dancing in some sort of pattern were a very good indicator to me that there was a lot more to explain than what I could learn in school or on television. While stargazing, moved by the potential of these suspended lights that visited me each night, I would travel in my imagination and lose myself in dreams of outer civilizations—the powerful creators of this system and its reigning entities. Was I curiously looking at the sky, or was I being called to pay attention, and to listen? Was I being called Home? Was the vast blackness watching me? Are we being monitored? Are we earthlings working for something larger without knowing it? I regularly wondered about these questions, and I loved to think of something—or someone—up there, tuning in, and dropping information.

On these nights, I somehow looked forward knowing that my life would be amazing. Well, life is amazing, but I defined *amazing* differently back then. I used to see myself as an astronaut, a Hollywood film star, or as a millionaire playboy always living the extreme. I imagined riding the wave of success, abundance, and happiness on a cheerful avenue of money. Beautiful woman, fast cars, yachts, and stunning castles. Laughing and enjoying life, I'd rest in the feeling of *I did it,* satisfied and accomplished.

After high school, I jumped in the fast lane and landed in the dark and deep world of drug abuse, descending down the spiral of addiction. I felt apart and different from everyone else at home or in school, not identifying with their principles, attitudes, or position in life. Drugs seemed to be my best friend and my best escape. I thought the drugs opened new possibilities too big to reject. I gladly let them lead me into new areas of philosophy, history, and life itself. They allowed me to explore the mind and its hidden doors of empirical knowledge, along with its windows of telepathic information, perception, and self-discovery.

It was a period of dramatic growth in consciousness that was difficult to catch up on in my reflected environment. Imagination led the way in all areas of my life, taking consciousness and awareness to unbelievable places that I knew to be true but were yet unspoken. I was in awe of the possibilities and excited with my ventures.

I was on an endless cosmic search. There were so many areas for growth and awareness, so much to find out, so much to discover. Practical life had to be more than what was going on with me or around me—or was I just too ambitious? Surely the energy that spins galaxies, creates stars, planets, and life, could continue to evolve and be much more powerful than this. (I'm that guy who believes teleportation is and will be a reality, common and accessible to those who want it, when we're ready!) Those days, in my mind, I often pictured that stream from the forest of my youth, with perfect life flourishing around it and a variety of species living together in harmony. I felt sure that we, too, could live like this: organic, easily flowing, thriving separately but together while connected with purpose and meaningful actions on a mission of peace in cooperation with the environment. I saw life as a vibration from space to the center of the earth, pouring over to us. The way plants come out of the soil could only be an example of its capacity to grow and to give. We, as an intelligent and rational species, need to guide this energy and harmony in the right direction, using it for progressive creating actions.

I continued searching for the way humans, or at least myself, could live to our full potential; healing powers, levitation, creativity, and free from all restrictions. I wanted one hundred percent of brain and intelligence usage. I wanted not only *more*—I wanted *it all*! But, like many others before and many after me, while on the quest for ultimate discovery, the day came when I hit rock bottom. At this stage, I could no longer fool myself, let alone anyone else. I was exhausted, beaten, and dead inside. With no friends or family around, I was sad with the result of my quest and lightly embarrassed by the consequences. But ... I did get my answers! It was not in vain. It was fruitful. But times had to change!

I saw no other way out besides getting myself into rehab, which I did with the help of my uncle. He had been to rehab himself in the late 80s, a successful case of *get clean, get up, and get going*. One afternoon, he saw me on the side of the road, stopped his car, opened the window, and called for me. I looked up to see that he was driving a beautiful, brand-new Bentley, light bluish in color with white leather interiors. He said, "Do you want to get out of here? Do you want to get better?" That question was music to my ears, and I immediately imagined elegant women, beautiful parties, lots of money, and a good quality of life! He had my full attention.

I was aware that my uncle had also experienced trouble at a young age, but here he was driving a Bentley. I thought, *He found a way; he knows how to get better.* I immediately replied to him, "Yes, I want to get well." But what I was really thinking was, *I want a Ferrari and a mansion with money and women.* He answered, "Okay, I'll pick you up in two days. We're going to England," and drove away.

I was left there on the road, thinking, *I'm going to London to get a job and get a life.* I had always wanted to go to London to study naval architecture, so I was excited, full of ideas, riding that wave and creating the momentum to turn my life around. That is, until I found out I was actually going to a rehab center for a seven-month program; a program to get me "clean and sober, one day at a time." What a raw deal! In all honesty, I didn't care. All I wanted was to get out of the streets. Anything was better than where I had been previously.

However, I must admit, to my total surprise, the program was fantastic. The people were kind, warm, loving, and caring. They understood me, they knew exactly where I was coming from, and they patiently guided me through the rough process of sober growth. It was a fantastic experience. I had time to consider the mechanisms of life, thought with feelings, and the healing power of love and acceptance through human interaction. The program guided me in a study of the *self,* to understand why I was sick, and to ask why was I killing myself. The main goal was to learn to master your mind and emotions so you can begin making wise decisions that will change your results. "Your best thinking got you here" was a phrase used often. But first, we had to share our thoughts and feelings with the group. How good is that?

In meetings, ten people would focus on you, your feelings, and consequentially, on correcting or redirecting your thinking in a healthier direction. After all, our actions are ultimately based on our feelings, which are a consequence of how we act upon circumstances. These actions are related to our understanding of the situation, our perspective, our awareness of what we consider to be reality, and ultimately to our core beliefs that our subconscious mind has been programmed since a young age to accept. The entire mechanism that creates our choices in day-to-day life was exposed, addressed, and corrected. It was a unique and satisfying experience to have a few hours of the day focused on resetting or re-educating the mind. It was a therapeutic, educational re-engineering of my mind so that I could live well and thrive. It was amazing and I was loving it. I now understood what was pushing me on this a self-destructive path, and why. I learned the kind of information that can sort you out for life. It worked for me. During my stay, I learned, understood, and valued the meaning of gratitude. I found *gratitude* to be a safe place that you can go to at any time, any hour of any day, for as long as you wish. It is a loving place that will hug you within minutes of arriving there.

It was hard work, my emotional and self-analytic journey. I was introduced for the second time in my life to the great reality that, indubitably, we are solely and fully responsible for our lives and any of our results. I had created my own reality, and now I was being given a chance to stop, review, and create an even better one. Gratitude was the base foundation.

This new realization completely changed the way I thought. We are the creators of our path through our thoughts, our perceptions, our desires, actions and our expectations. It was interesting to discuss and develop these sorts of concepts with the other visionaries, dreamers, and unconventional thinkers that I met in rehab. People who question their rights and options and stand up against difficult circumstances. From all sorts of backgrounds and many countries, we came together to discuss feelings, reason, options, the opportunity of life, and to expand our minds in order to find new solutions. It was nothing short of amazing.

The rich, the poor, the old, the young, the gay, the straight, the punk, the artist, the money maker, the nightclub dancer, the housewife, the party people—you name it. In that room was a representative from every corner of society, and most of them were ready to quit drugs and find a better life. Such a powerful connection forged from the common awareness of our potential.

Chemical dependency is a bitch. It's hard, and no one needs it. Or maybe some do need it to get them to where they need to be, to a place of change. Whatever the case, I knew I didn't want it anymore. I was done with it, tired and exhausted from the mental and physical battle that had taken too much of me.

It had slowly smoked away my soul as I staggered down a dead-end path. I had a good run, though. It was fun in the beginning, but now I was done with it.

When focused on recovery, I found prayer and meditation essential to walking the right path in a positive and clean manner. The healing and creative powers of meditation are still essential to my well-being, and its powers are undeniable and of incredible value. Besides being the absence of thought, it is your soul's reconnection, recognizing its place and recalling its creative power in the universe. It's your consciousness accepting guidance from the Supreme Intelligence, and together, creating the new desired path for life experience. It is having faith: believing in the unseen and expecting it to happen to you; believing in something you can only see in your mind's eye; asking and believing that you have received it; being grateful for it, feeling it, loving it, and releasing your vision with love into the ether. Praying is not necessarily getting down on your knees and talking to an imaginative figure in the sky, but if that works for you, great!

Recovery is all about faith, independent of religion. It is believing that we can have what we deeply desire. It's believing that we deserve and will have a better life, independent of opinions! And the system works, so it will deliver what we really want, period. And it does—all of it! I think of faith as that intuition that whispers to you, "You can have it," each time you follow your conscious and take inspired action. Faith inspires you to get up and get going, to chase your dreams, to take ownership of your desired dream. We all want a happy, abundant, and fulfilled life. Faith is believing you have received it already! It's yours. "Ask, and it is given." Again, whatever works for you is good, too! That's the beauty of life; we can all play according the same laws but yet reach different conclusions. Because it's *law*, it works, so we don't have to worry! This brings me to the first Universal Law I began to study, the Law of Thinking: *We can only attract the things we think about.* The power of this law by itself solves the world's biggest problems! If we take our time, repeat it to ourselves and believe it with all we've got from early morning to late night, you can have a life that is nothing short of fantastic! This concept raised my awareness to higher levels every day and each time I used it. It lifted my mood, my feelings, my perspective on life and my expectations. Now, I believed I could expect to have a life experience in resonance with my new thoughts! I knew I was working on it, and I knew I was creating my own reality with joy, with love, and with laughter. This time no one could take it from me, or even take credit for it! By changing my thought patterns, I changed my results. This was my new job, to think well of myself and think about what I want. Easy!

After a year of being clean and sober, I couldn't have been more joyful. My entire perspective on life had changed, and I was filled with positive expectations. Amazed with my experience in rehab, I felt complete. I felt I had qualified, done my time, and paid my bills in the dark side so that I could now enjoy a brighter happy life. Multiple daily sessions of working on myself in group therapy was tremendously effective. It was a fantastic healing process to have a variety of other souls listening, attending, caring, and helping to process life. I did the same for them; it was a reciprocal procedure, hence its magnificent efficiency, and we all benefitted from the honesty and love we'd given each other. Still, besides its amazing powers and my immense gratitude, I wanted more. There was something in me eager to create and seek excitement. I was forever grateful as I had a new me and new possibilities—including a normal life— but that was still not enough. This transformation had helped me a great deal, but it only opened my mind to the abundance of potential in the world. It opened the perception of possibility, and with it, an awareness of the endless energy of being. I wanted more.

This stage of my life came in tune with the second Universal Law that I later studied, the Law of Supply: *The universe is an unlimited source of supply. There is enough for everyone. Ask, and it is given. Believing is seeing. Thoughts become realities.*

In the asking, it is given. This belief that we can have, do, and be all that we want, working together with the Law of Thinking, was the front door to the kingdom of unlimited growth— and I had just stepped through it. The power of this concept is unlimited, and I was just beginning to grasp it! Immediately, my imagination began spinning thinking of instinctive dreams and wishes yet to fulfil. There would be no limits: I could finally focus and chase my ideals as the universe would supply what I would require, again, independently of opinion. That was very empowering for me. At the same time, this concept matched with the second step in the rehab program that states: "We came to believe that a power greater than ourselves could restore us to sanity." In my case, this went straight up to the stars, to the night sky—that was my Higher Power reference, as nothing could beat the power of a starry sky. Right away, I started writing down goals and desires for the future.

Now that I was sober and had a clear mind, I felt the potential of my gifts as a human participant. My spirit, my oversoul, my essence had resurfaced. It took over the entire set with responsibility and conscious awareness, free again, ready to take this body into new experiences, unclouded by the misjudgment of drugs. I could see their benefits in the expansion and acceptance of possibilities, but now I was happy with clarity and with having power over the collected knowledge. I am naturally a relentless spirit that always wants something. I can sit and relax, but not for long. Some new idea will pop up, something will trigger my curiosity, and I find no reason not to explore it. Astrologists say it's my regent planet Uranus—unsettled! Whatever they decided to call that mixture of energy that influenced the origin, I resonate with.

After rehab, I had control over my thoughts, my words, and, most importantly, my actions. It was my second time experiencing a real, life-assuring moment of self-power, self-control, and self-definition. The first experience had been under the heavy influence of psychedelics, and you can never be quite sure if that's reliable information or not. When we're high, we think we're right, we know we're right, and we see what we feel. Then, we find that we're talking to a moving tree as the moon pops up to say hello from a wobbly, fractal, starry sky, and we ask ourselves, "Did that just happen?" This becomes our new normal, living in an animated sensory field where emotions have colors, densities, and frequencies. It was amazing, and I guess that's why I stayed there for so long!

After seven months of intense psychotherapy, my day of release had arrived. I was grateful for the process. I felt confident to move forward, eager to experience life through my new filters. Sober, loving, peaceful, in a constant high of the vibrations of positive thought. Excitement with a surprise factor—*expectancy*—that's the word I'm looking for! I was loved and cared for, and I could feel it, mostly because I loved and cared for myself.

I forgave myself for all my past mistakes. The past is the past, with nothing but learning and good memories to take from it. I was now in the real world and had true friends. I was detached from the collective madness and even with nothing to my name, I was looking forward to experiencing life in my new suit.

It was greatly rewarding to feel human again. The spontaneity and honesty of the present moment was very refreshing. The warm feeling of connecting with people on the same or higher frequency reassured me that I was on the right path, or at least on a better path. I was going somewhere, to a place better than before. Though I was unsure where I was going, I knew exactly how to get there: staying clean, sober, sharing, meditating, reading, studying, loving, and respecting. Leading up to build well, it couldn't go wrong. And here, the Law of Attraction started to deliver the *better*. I was acknowledging better results, as I was consciously getting myself into a better mindset and better attitude. I had clear well-intended thoughts associated with good feelings, and so one after the other, the occurrence of similar beneficial episodes kept coming. Life was getting better, with intention. I was having fun, feeling well, meeting positive people, and advancing in interesting mental concepts focused on well-being through life experiences, either for others or for myself.

As per the Law of Attraction: *What we focus on, we will attract. Everything we experience in our lives is dictated by our own mind. We must think of what we want and emotionalize it to bring it into our experience.* This is the second piece of the Law of Vibration: *Vibrations of the same frequency resonate with each other. Like energy attracts like energy.* So, as we select our vibration through our thoughts, we're dictating what level of vibrational situations, people, and things we attract to experience next, giving us full control over our lives. This was a crucial step for what I see today as my personal development. Taking care of my life experience through conscious thought patterns. And so, it was! I got myself in an incredible *good mood* vibration and the universe delivered me more situations to match that feeling. It's beautiful because it works!

I was following all the suggestions for a successful recovery: attending meetings, doing service (by *service* I mean we take care of others; helping in nursing homes, serving coffee in meetings, or even sharing messages of hope in prisons), and working the steps. I got a job and was a responsible member of society, at least trying to fit in (once again) and not being the old rag that I was in past days. I was working at a printing factory, carrying large sheets of paper for outdoor banners, changing paint trays, and transporting large rolls of paper. Machines were punching and puffing all day in a rustic industrial environment where I didn't want to be. It was fun to see how everything worked, but I had lost interest after a week!

I did what I was told, helping to rearrange the templates for printing. I was being paid six hundred dollars a month and paying all my own bills. Getting up at five o'clock each morning,

I'd catch a bus at six to be at work at seven. This was a first for me. I had never been through this process before. It was an eye opener, sharing the bus with mostly older people carrying fish, fruits, and items from the market. Persisting in order to integrate into society took effort. I found myself looking around and thinking, *Man ... we (as in humanity) can do so much better than this.* But I kept going. I had to grow into the new person I wanted to become, reliable, trustworthy, and independent. So far, I was doing way better than following my own head. I recently read this quote: "You don't need to fit in, we're not here for long." Isn't this beautiful? Bring out your essence and let us know you. Today, I believe there is a time for everything!

I was utilizing the benefits of meditation and waiting for answers before deciding what to do or where to go. This was essential for my well-being. Listening to my intuition became a recurrent habit; connecting to a higher self was now a daily practice. At night, I experienced how powerful a good review of the day and a meditation can be. After reviewing the day's events, I'd imagine the next day, idealizing how I would want it all to go. Taking the time to preview would definitely make a difference for the next day's results, boosting my self-confidence in the process.

As I read recently, "Prayer is part of the process of a desired creation from the ether on to the physical world." This is not religion, it is metaphysics. It's important to remove the paradigms and pre-concepts of traditional society. Prayer as a form of meditation is a tool based on gratitude. It allows you to find out where you are and bring you to where you want to be, which is at one with your essence and desires. This understanding allowed me to find tremendous benefits in preparing the next day's to-do lists, where to go, who to see, how to speak, and how to work towards my desired results. It was now easy to understand the concept of cause and effect, so I was finding and dictating the causes for my desired effects. This idea by itself is another Universal Law—the Law of Cause and Effect: *For every effect there is a definite cause. Likewise, for every cause, there is a definite effect. Be a cause for what you want, and you will get the effect. Your thoughts, behaviors, and actions create specific effects that manifest and create your life as you know it.*

This was new to me. Previously, I had been spontaneous, letting the wind carry me along and see where it would take me according to circumstances. But from this point on, I added efficiency to my day and my own signature with the power of choice and decision. At that time, I had little money, no means, and only one chance to get what I wanted. I couldn't miss an opportunity, so I would plan in advance to make it happen. I was becoming a cause for the effect that I wanted. I was praying for guidance from the stars, the sky, the universe, the Supreme Intelligence, or the entire cosmos, to give me a chance, to help me position myself. From there, I could find the best actions to take, choosing my life, my desires and what mattered to me. I knew I could do better. I was very excited with this phase.

If we do our part, the universe responds in abundant ways. A very good friend and mentor once said to me, "Give one step to the universe, and the universe will give ten steps back to you." This was the best lesson on universal abundance because it is true. So, I adapted what seemed to be an invite to courage as a way of living. I did all I was asked and more, and the universe kept giving back. I had tremendous gratitude that life was developing in a positive sequence, getting richer, growing clean and healthy. I could start from fresh, and I knew it. As another good friend and mentor often says, "You are one decision away from a completely different life, if you believe." How empowering is that? How freeing and exciting! Add courage to it and you can become whoever you always wanted to be!

We all can, whenever we choose to do so.

Chapter 1

The Switch

From the darkest moment came the brightest solution.

n writing this book, my desire is to bring you awareness and knowledge of different experiences that may help you lay the foundation for a bright life with a solid future. Everyone has a different perspective, experience, and point of connection with this universe, with life, and with our planet. I want to share mine; who knows, it might amuse you!

We can always change our current circumstances with a change of perspective; I believe that to be the main benefit of thinking. By reassessing any situation, we can find a better way. "When we change the way we look at things, those things change" I don't remember who said that, but best-selling author and motivational speaker, Wayne Dyer, uses the phrase it a lot. And no wonder why—it's a very powerful truth. That which *is* does not necessarily have to *be*. There is no way we have to be. We can choose. That is the Law of Vibration at work again. What we believe, it is true. How we vibrate attracts like things into it. We don't need to worry; we just need to alter our perspective and attract a different reality. It's scientifically understood that thoughts have electromagnetic charges. Thoughts are things, and become things. Everything in this world is energy and we have a creative part in the reality that we experience. Maybe you are more powerful than what you were led to believe.

Consider my early life. I was sleeping in cars, dealing drugs, and running away from society. I had no control over my thoughts. I was truly broken and alone, without direction, guidance, or love. Why? *Perspective.* The Law of Relativity states: *Nothing is what it is until you relate it to something. Nothing is good or bad until it is related to something else, it's just relative. We are the ones who make something good or bad by comparing it to everything around us, so it is dependent on what the observer is it relating to. The nature, quality, or value of something can only be measured in relation to another object.* Perspective of the world around me influenced my choices, which led to reactions that were based on emotions. I was reacting. I wasn't allowing myself to see the beauty and purity in or around me. Knowledge and perspective change our lives, and that's how I became so grateful during this period. Grateful for the powers in me. I had a fresh and new perspective on myself and in my life potential. Recovery had given me a brand-new self-image, changed my core beliefs, value, self-love, and choice. I had full faith, both in myself and in the system.

I became content as I turned my life around, finding a solid, grounded way forward. It felt as if I could make the unthinkable happen. I was lighter, happier, and even if still broke at times, at least I was sleeping on a comfortable bed in a room with a roof! Gratitude started to grow, and the belief that I was doing well was multiplying my zest for life. All was well. However, I will never forget the period I spent without heat in a freezing room out of town. I froze my ass off, praying my circumstances would soon change. That moment changed me as a person. I had to put my feet in the sink with hot water just to avoid frostbite. But hey, at least I had hot water!

This was early in my recovery period, straight out of the rehab center's supportive community and into the real world. Now that I was sober, dealing with personal struggles was a lot easier. I had caring friends and loving people around me everywhere, proving another empiric truth: *When you love yourself, people will love you.* I had the job at the printing factory, which enabled me to pay my feeble rent. I also had peers from the group meetings. But most importantly, I had myself. I was calm and peaceful. I could think straight. I was in no rush. I had clothes on my back and places to go. I could take a shower, eat three meals a day, meet new people, enjoy activities, meet girls, go out for coffee, and enjoy connecting. This may sound like small stuff to you, but it was huge for me at the time.

This stage allowed me to feel at least other two of the Universal Laws that were operating daily on me! The Law of Polarity: *Everything that exists has an equal and exact opposite.* In a different vocabulary, the Law of Polarity states: *Polar opposites are what make existence possible. If what you aren't did not coexist with what you are, then what you are couldn't be.* In that cold freezing room, I knew deep inside that somewhere there existed an immensely comfortable, spacious, and warm room for me—it had to be! On a beach house in California, or perhaps Mexico, it was there, waiting for me! If it was that cold in this room, where was all the heat, and where were all the warm houses? They were on the opposite side; the opposite side of my previous choices—the opposite side of where I was! This night was my fuel to pursue the opposite of what I had been up until that day. Instead of cold, I was now in search warmth and comfort, and I never stopped! I use this law every day and always look for the positive side of any event, because it's there.

On the other hand, I was heavily working with the Law of Increase: *Be happy and grateful for what you have now, and you'll make it better. At the same time, believe that you can have more of it and let it grow. The key principle being gratefulness. Give praise for the good things and amplify them in our lives.* What you focus on, you will increase. That's what I was seriously holding on to! Based on the recovery rule that states, "A grateful addict doesn't need drugs," I was seriously holding on to and appreciating the small things that I should be happy and grateful for. I was appreciating them every day, every hour, or even by the minute. I knew my life had changed for better by that much in only one year since I became sober, and I knew the more I focused on it, the better it was becoming.

I went from being in a jail cell to enjoying a warm cup of coffee by the ocean with good friends. I was swapping galaxies. I was trading deep, dark spaces for a bright light of energy. It was a huge step. This change in my circumstances was proof that we can all change our lives. If I did it, so can anyone!

To do so, we must have gratitude first and foremost! Then, we must have faith and a desire to follow a new direction. I used those principles at base camp to get up and get going. I needed help, and I took it. I did all that was suggested to get out of where I was and head in the direction of where I wanted to be. It worked. Yet, I was missing something, and I couldn't quite put my finger on it. The recipe was missing an ingredient, and it didn't take me long to determine what that missing ingredient was: *discipline*. Taking control to see things through to the end, to finish tasks, to actually do what needs done.

One of my favorite teachers in Law of attraction and Personal Development describes *discipline* as: *Giving an order to yourself and following it.* This made a huge difference. The resulting productivity is enormous, and this was the early 2000s when cell phones were not yet smart! You'd use them to make phone calls, occasional texts, and that was it! Even then, it was easy to get side-tracked, discarding the steps needed to achieve your goals. Today, I take this even more seriously. Make a plan and follow it until it's complete or nothing will happen, because no one else will complete it for you! The rewards are worthy! The feeling of achieving has no match! It's ours—our credit and our prize to reclaim.

In one of his mentoring programs, along with many subjects, we focused repeatedly on developing our mental faculties: perception, reason, will, memory, imagination, and intuition. Each one by itself could lead to a few paragraphs in description and appreciation of its importance, but I mentioned this because I made a decision to apply discipline in evolving my mental faculties. They are the foundation for the creative process. I believed that if I developed these mental faculties, I wouldn't need to worry about anything else as they can dictate our beliefs, actions, expectations and assumptions, creating our future self and consequent experiences. I found it of tremendous importance.

By doing so, we can achieve whatever we think, whatever we want. But we must have the desire. We must want it, *really* want it, to make the wheels of magic spin. Having the desire to do it, to have it, and to be it, is imperative. The burning desire to have it all! Nothing could stop me.

I felt as if I was a in a raw state and wanted to create a newer, even better personality. Like buying a new, wide-open piece of land and letting your mind run free, wondering what type of house to create from scratch. I'd whipped out from the old outcast within me. I was letting go of rebellion, swapping it for the acceptance of the peaceful idea of joining a running system. This was a big deal, as I'd always been part of the resistance. When you're an outcast, you experience a strong sense of *us versus them*. Defend the poor, fight the system, erase corruption, protest and fight—I was done with it all. No more spending energy on anything other than creating a positive scenario for myself. I knew that if I wanted to change the world, I would first have to change myself into the person I wanted to see in it.

As drug addicts, first we get kicked out of society, and then we run even further away from it. We blame others—our friends, family, or even the government. Anything can be a source of blame. We do this instead of taking responsibility for our actions, and we tend to develop a strong sense of *good and bad* or *right and wrong*. Those harsh opinions create even more separation and conflict instead of the *peace and love* that we once stood for.

Back then, I saw the system as a corrupt machine of obedient people following someone else's plan for enrichment without asking crucial questions: Where we were going? What are we doing with our resources? What is our real role and potential on earth? The truth is, only a small group would question the system, and this reality was infuriating to me. *Was it just me? Was I crazy? I think they're deluded ... should I tell them? Is it the chemicals? Am I the deluded one?* Perhaps I had to be on drugs opening doors of perception to think something else was out there involving us all in this cosmic picture. Maybe I should keep these thoughts to myself, so no one finds out. Being an addict doesn't have much of a silver lining, but you definitely have time to think in some very creative states of mind.

Do we remain ignorant about our position on the planet or in the cosmos? Within society, we crave general culture and academic knowledge, but we fall short in using our abilities and realizing our potential. They are not the same, but rather, complementary constructs. How do people accept conformity? How do they wake up, commute in traffic, work a job they don't like, accept a low salary, and remain content in a world of mediocrity? This used to drive me mad. I wanted to wake everyone up. I wanted to drop LSD in the main water supply and turn on all the taps all at once. I wanted to drop acid in their food and open the gates of love and understanding for the masses. I wanted to shake our country in the light of love, creativity, and compassion to then rise in greatness and joy. It's with love and joy I see how much we know today about this topic. It excites me. I know change is here now.

Now, let's be fair. There are happy, successful people and families who are motivated and moving forward within the laws of the universe without needing anyone to teach them. They have their jobs, their cars, and houses, and it's loveable—bless them! Any bringers of joy, peace and happiness are welcome in my book! Any happy soul is a gift to the universe. They are in tune with the great motives of mankind and are proud carriers of the torch. These are the scientists, doctors, engineers, musicians, writers, and thinkers; they are the many good-hearted people who have pushed civilization forward in a positive direction. They are in alignment with the great design, with the expression and expansion of the Supreme Intelligence. I am profoundly grateful to them. I salute all the extraordinarily successful and stubborn minds that kept going because they believed they were doing it right, regardless of the opinion of others. Thank you. Well done! You inspire us all to grow.

I guess I just wanted more. Finding out that we get what we choose out of life, I wondered, do the masses know about this? Shouldn't this principle be taught in school? What would happen if we pushed our children to meditate from a young age, to think about what makes them truly happy, to consider the life they'd like to live, to think about what they want, and to focus on *having it already*. This would be brilliant; kids would love to learn in a classroom setting like this, using their imagination in full power and freedom of choice.

The fact is, we have a platform whereby we can grow and develop into anything we want, and that's a great achievement for us all. Like the Mayans predicted, a certain period came to an end in 2012. Since then, extra energy and light protons have inhabited our planet, bringing enlightenment to all corners of the earth. Why? Because we are now getting in closer range of another star, which is feeding us alongside our main star, the Sun. As a result, we get more light and pure love energy. We're inevitably gaining a feeling of belonging and becoming. We're more vibrant as we're drawn towards the clarification that we are powerful creators.

The Zenith is near. As a consequence of this new clarity, we are exchanging dark and obscure practices for a life filled with light, elevating mankind to operate with better practices, clearer intentions, and more extreme honesty. We can now manifest our true intentions and objectives and pick our fruits regardless of opinion. We know our part. We're connecting with the cosmos, enlightened by the spirit of our origins and the force that creates worlds and keeps us spinning in the black space of our universe with love, excitement, and joy.

Only We Hold Ourselves Back

As we take steps in the chosen direction, the universe responds with its open doors as an invitation to creative imagination. It's obvious when the universe replies to our efforts: you can feel an abundance of energy through endless sessions of exciting sketches, plans, and ideas. The joy of a new idea fuels our mental activity allowing us to take fearless action, assuming our dreams will come true. The moment where magic happens and you become who you dream to be by assuming, by calling it into you, now (the Law of Assumption). Some say this the most important law, as your assumptions are based on what you believe, think, and feel! This is the basis for creating your reality because when you assume that it is, only then can it be. Hence the power of these magical moments of imagining and dreaming your life away!

Neville Goddard states regularly in his books and lectures that, "Assumptions have the power of objective realization. Every event in the visible world is the result of an assumption or idea in the unseen world." So, assume the feeling of your wish already being fulfilled and the Law of Assumption will bring it into being. It will. As we take steps in the direction of our dreams, we must take momentum, grab the magic, and assume it's already happening. As we allow this energy in us, we connect and allow perfection to come in. Life jumps forward, we feel better, we dream so clearly that it feels real and we believe in our core. We win! Not against anyone, but against our own minds. The ego fights back for survival, mostly because it hangs on the old paradigms and tries to keep you safe from hurting yourself in the risk-taking decisions of life. It wants you to believe that the old methods were better and truer, shutting down the new you. It does this to keep you safely in your comfort zone, and this is where we must rise again and hold onto that excitement of the dream being fulfilled. I love this.

Luckily for us, by then, it's already too late for the ego to win. You've seen the light and connected to the source of all life with the clarity of the future moment where you manifested it in your visions. You felt it. It's engraved in your mind's eye, your soul knows it, and that's the feeling you must keep holding on to. It requires a decision to keep it and the persistence to maintain the image and the vibration that elevates you to your birth right place of abundance and plenitude on earth. It's yours! Cherish it, love it, keep it.

The fact is, you now know and see a better way to live. Once you start tasting it, it will get even better. It requires work to keep it, but with practice, it gets easier and easier to maintain the high, untroubled vibration. The rewards are immense and impossible to ignore. Abundance kicks in, the Law of Attraction brings more of it, and people and events are working into realizing your dreams with ease, allowing for anything to happen.

We're stardust, all connected to the stars. How can we settle for living in pain when such great opportunity to find release is available? Why would we have to struggle? It doesn't make sense. There is more to be fulfilled in life. It is freely given to us in the first place. Why make it so hard and so expensive these days to just *be*?

My goal as I reintegrated into society was to stop fighting and just go with the flow, to just be normal. What does that even mean? Around 2001 was my attempt to be "a normal guy." Rebellion had fueled my chemical-dependent days, and that was in the past. If I was to achieve any healing, any growth and expansion into something I had never been before, I needed to grasp and understand the natural forces of the earth and humanitarian causes. I needed to grasp the natural ways of just *being*. I was happy with the idea of simply being naturally human; after all, my rebellious, hippie-ish alienated ways didn't work out well the first time around. I now surrendered to the larger force fields, asked for help, and soaked up guidance. I made a request to the civilized world: S*how me how to live on your terms!*

On society's terms, on the terms of the masses. To mix in the crowd, be normal, get a haircut, get a nine-to-five, watch TV, and be content. Even if I was boiling inside with desire for more, for extremes, and for excitement (as is my nature), I was willing and humbled, ready to follow direction and to obey—so I thought!

With sobriety you gain clarity in many areas that were previously unseen, and one of them was having a satisfying feeling of instant karma—a daily proof that my actions were fully responsible for my results. Cause and effect straight out of my creation, and I loved it! I was done with blaming everyone for everything, and it was such a relief. It was all me and me alone. I was ready, willing, and able to take responsibility. I finally felt like an adult, grown up and connected to the civilized world. I was part of the grand scheme of things and observed an immediate response from life. It was like using a joystick in a video game. I could be the good guy now, playing successfully, doing the right thing, and scoring positive results.

Building a Meaningful Life

We strive to create a meaningful life, regardless of what each of us consider to be meaningful. While taking a moral inventory, looking at my successes and failures, the good times along with the times of learning, I realized the specific steps I could now take to emerge in a wonderful version of my own life. I discovered fundamental building blocks that position us all for a connected, meaningful, and fulfilling life. Putting these blocks in place takes a decision, focus, and yes, discipline. It's a joyous process, and nothing comes to your experience without you energizing it in the first place. You are always utilizing energy, sometimes in positive deliberate form, sometimes random, and sometimes on autopilot.

Thus, why not choose the energy that is to your benefit? Why not channel the unlimited amount of energy you have in order to create? Why not focus to make a difference in your life, and consequently, in the lives of those around you? I want to help you do that, and I believe that the following elements will position you to sculpt a meaningful life.

Planning

Making plans fires up all of our mental faculties, but mostly imagination, which creates amazing results. I decided that each evening I would review that day, looking for ways to improve or do better the next day. I could foresee the day's episodes in my mind: the challenging moments, the winning points, the learning curves, the creation of goals, and finally, the laughter and enjoyment from the success of a fruitful day.

What kind of personality did I bring? Was I arrogant or was I kind? Had I shown my best self, or had I played an uninspired role? Was I in touch with my inner self? Was I used, or had I been tricked? Did I make the right choices? Did I spend the day with genuine friends? Was I spontaneous? Through reflection, I assembled the right plan for the following day: who was I going to meet? And when that happens, who will I be? How will I reply? Will I laugh, talk, or listen? Knowing our tendencies to react to emotions rather than responding with clarity, I found that creating a good rapport with the intervenient would bring benefits to all. "Be the change you want to see," said Gandhi. And so, I tried. I tried to the most of my abilities and it felt pretty great.

I played each scene back and forth in my mind until I found an answer. I wanted to sleep well, with a clear conscience and reinforced character, as dealing correctly with other human beings was one of my main goals. Needless to say, it was well worth it.

I looked at all the possible ways a conversation might go. This allowed me to be prepared for any and all surprises that life could send my way. I felt safe and observed positive results from this time of reflection. I tinkered, adjusted, and toyed with my behavior. Everything was intentional, and the results were amazing. I could feel it; people would be impressed and caught off guard, taking my assertiveness as proof of reliability and intention. I didn't mean to, I just wanted to be ready and make the most of our encounter. That was new to me, and it proved that a little bit of planning goes a very long way.

Visualization

To supplement planning, I visualized my ideal scenarios, constantly trying to foresee my desired results. This works like a charm because it removes diversions from the outset, eliminating the factor of surprise to a great extent. I got this advice from my counsellor who had been sober from hard drugs for 25 years and who had an immense knowledge of human behavior, psychology, emotions, mind hacks—as well as giant heart. He is a brilliant human with a hard sense of humor. He suggested, "Reflect on it, and work where it's needed to improve by visualizing the changes in motion." I guess I had already been doing it unconsciously, but now it was with clarity, focus, and intention. Visualizing also helped by raising the quality and the vibration of each encounter or situation as I could live the emotions and make them better for the next time.

Knowing

There's a Chinese proverb that I live by, "If a problem has a solution, why worry? If the problem doesn't have a solution, why worry?" In short, there are no real problems. Knowing this can solve all of our problems. This idea requires growth and belief, but it does create solutions. Feel it. Believe it. Perspective. There are no problems, only our resistance to the most immediate result and the emotional charges that we chose to hold on to. There are narratives that we choose to validate. What we focus on we make bigger, utilizing our invisible powers of thought. The mind can be our best friend or our strongest enemy, so we need to keep it in check and make it work for us as our best-ever buddy.

This brings me straight to one of my favorite Universal Laws: The Law of Perpetual Transmutation of Energy: *All energy is in motion and all energy that is in motion will eventually appear in the physical form. Thoughts transmuted into physical form. Meaning, because our thoughts are energy, they will eventually appear in the physical form.* This is how we have the ability to change our life and reality. I love this law; it gives us control once again and full responsibility for any of our results and life experiences. What you focus on, you bring about. What you energize, you grow. Focus on what you want and think about the good things. They're not clichés, they're wisdom. I love knowing that I'm worthy of my choices, because I am worthy of anything I choose and desire to experience. Think about what you want, love it, and allow it to come to you because it's well worth it. Use your gifts and take your prize because it's yours for the taking, and visualizing it will bring it to the table faster. Choose the ideal outcome, but be specific and detailed. Every aspect of your desired experience should be taken into account; don't leave anything to the decision of others. After all, it's *your* life that you're designing—so choose well!

Through visualizing, I forecast and project my ideals to the world, into the ether of creation, letting the universe know what life I want, feeling the emotion of the outcome that I desire, because thoughts are powerful creative energy. My ideal life exists and holds a vibrational signature. It has an identity, and I can feel it. I can tune into it and shift into that reality becoming the person I want to be. So, all I need to do is meet that. In doing so, I feel my body accepting this outcome as reality. It becomes part of my story; it is written in my gallery of time and space, and I subconsciously move in its direction. *Be and act like the person you want to be, and you will become that person.* Be in the vibration of what you want and let it come to you. All of this is based in the universal laws, of attraction, of assumption, of perpetual transmutation of energy, and vibration. I love it because you create your own reality!

It's a simple process. I close my eyes and focus solely on my breath: deep breaths in and deep breaths out, breath by breath, until I'm thoughtless. I feel my body relax and now

I'm in an elevated state. Images begin flashing and I intuitively start visualizing in accordance with my honest and deepest desires! Embracing the universal creative presence, appreciating it, loving it.

With my eyes still closed, I visualize the moments I want to experience. I look around, using all my senses. I can feel the moment. I imagine how it will make me feel, how I want to feel experiencing the things that I desire, laughing, loving; In doing so, I program my mind to strive for that moment, to expect it to happen. And, magically, the next day, I take every action I can to make it a true reality.

Spirit

When in doubt (when I disconnect), I ask for guidance from inside to remove anything that may be clouding my thoughts and allow me to reconnect. You don't have to be Christian, Hindu, or any other religion at all to believe in a Higher Power. Something that is ... I wouldn't like to say *superior* to ourselves, as we're part of it, but something or someone that is definitely calmer and more knowledgeable than us. We can easily be distracted on a daily basis. The world and the universe keep proving, day-by-day, that an exceptional level of intelligence is operating around us and we have no idea how far it goes. If we are not focused, connected, or in touch with the inner self, we'll inevitably prove ourselves to be unaware of less than well-intended energy. Part of humanity is a kind of destroyer with no apparent reason. It's a direction I can't always understand, but it's correcting itself by now in the direction of a peaceful world.

As such, it's up to us by looking within to design and create *In Spirit* the path we want for ourselves. A path we'll be proud to look back on, a message or a legacy to leave behind. With this in mind, it becomes easier to believe in a higher power or entity. Let's call it God, the Grand Overall Design, this Powerful Energy or Supreme Intelligence that evolved from Being itself and has created worlds and galaxies, and where we are now to know itself. Keeping in mind that this can also be only one of its types of expressions. This is what we can see. We are the players on this game, but who knows how many games were created out there at the same time? Keep in mind that there are many other substances and expressions that we cannot see, smell, taste, or touch; there are unlimited options. I do believe that who or whatever created this playground for us has the power and ability to do much more. This creative force, energy, or universal consciousness has come all the way from outer space to the Spirit within us, we are It, here to experience life as we want, and as we choose it. That which we manifest, that which we experience, becomes something we grow with, and grow for, when it pleases us. In contrast, we blame God when it doesn't please us.

We look to God when we don't understand some aspect of life, religion, or science. We accept that we evolved from the monkeys, which makes no sense as monkeys are still monkeys, but maybe it was a gift or reward, and everyone's happy to leave it at that. We trust an unknown force is behind or above us all deciding what we get next, well it's not. It's here expanding with us. Its existence is not for us to admit it or not, but it helps if we recognize it's there, allowing us to grow and be part of it. Connect, let it show you what it can do through you and not to you, as you are part of it. Remember the beautiful Serenity Prayer: "God, grant me the serenity to accept the things I cannot change, the courage to change the things I can, and the wisdom to know the difference." We could replace *God* with *Spirit*, *Life*, *Knowledge*, or *Supreme Intelligence*. It is the presence that guides our best judgment, grants calmness, and instills peace of mind that makes us do good.

This prayer has a magical effect, relieving us from the pressure, guilt, or obligation for control that the collective mind imposes on us. Say it out loud, and just like that—snap—problems solved. It's a chill pill for the moments when we're struggling with doubt or fear. Whatever is giving you a hard time is only a creation within your creation. It's a narrative, a perspective, and it can always be changed. When this is true, the solution starts inside your mind as well. It starts with you, and with a decision to change. Just let it go, and it will be gone!

I know Spirit is perfect, pure energy, love, all-knowing Universal Intelligence and creative joy. If I allow it to flow through me, there's joy instead of problems, love, and no worries—only happiness in life and better things to come.

Remove Your Worry

Worry only comes to us when we call to it. It's an invitation to problems, so don't invite them!

Let go of worry! We create it and open the door for worry to walk through; then, the more we dwell on it, the more it grows until it looks like a huge problem. Otherwise, it wouldn't be there. We need to let it go and trust the perfect universe that everything is going to be okay, and that everything is working perfectly. By believing it will be okay, we're actually allowing it and inviting it to be okay! It's that easy. Remember, life grows easily within nature, and so it should be within us. If it's an answer for which we are searching, it will most likely come from within ourselves. But we have to let go of the problem in order to create space for the solution. Albert Einstein said, "We can't solve a problem with the same thinking that created it."

This brings another great Universal Law, the Law of Compensation: *The universe fills up the empty space or vacuum with the things that we desire.* Or put another way: *We are compensated in direct proportion to what we put out into the universe. Good happens in the space we give to it. Focus on the good, always.* This is another simple and rewarding law that works regardless of whether you believe it or not. Since I found the powerful impact of this law in my life, it gave a new meaning to the word *selfish.* Yes, I removed the negativity and worry from my mind so that I could create the space for joy, love, happiness, calmness and success to come. And you know what? It worked! I chose to give space to the good, and good came! And it keeps getting better and better because I work at it. As one of my favorite mentors says, "It's simple, but it's not easy!" To a child I would say, "We are all working in the same Life factory; we all need to put in our time creating the life that we want so that we might be able to get it. Otherwise, someone else will choose for you!"

Life works perfectly. Our nature is perfect, and a problem is but an observation, a perspective. Pema Chodron reminds us, "The mind is the source of all suffering, and it is also the source of all happiness." We have to let go of what's bothering us. Otherwise, it will keep bothering us. Easy! You have everything you need from birth, and I'm not talking about material possessions— I'm talking about the perfect expression of life.

The relief that comes with realizing that you have very little to worry about certainly makes the day better. When I admit that I cannot control what's beyond my power, or even beyond my interest to think about it, I am free to move forward and focus again on what I want, actually changing my life for the better. Even if you need help in decision-making, try meditating to get the answer. Or, if you're in a rush, the perspective of the Serenity Prayer works every time. It helps you remain focused and not waste time. It's a win-win situation. I've used it for many different subjects, and if the answer doesn't come immediately, it will show up once I allow it to. It always works, and it never fails. I'm not religious and I believe there are beneficial tools in many areas of human operation. Neil de Grasse Tyson said (and I love this quote), "If a discussion lasts longer than five minutes, both sides are wrong." I use this notion in discussions with myself, knowing that I need to let it go. The answer will come naturally.

Putting the *Zen* in Zenith

As I distanced from my addiction and became healthier, happier and stronger emotionally, I started wanting more. Growth gave space for it. I wished for more and hoped for more. I didn't want to work in a factory. I was grateful, but not content. I was both dissatisfied with where I was in life and grateful that I could change. It was a great lesson for me. Some people receive this valuable lesson earlier in their lives, while others never receive it at all. I certainly had the benefit of perspective.

As an exit move from that scenario, I enrolled in an IT/AV & Computer Programming course paid for by the government as an initiative to create knowledge and inform those who desired. Life immediately got better. Not only was I making more money, but I was also learning and stretching my brain activity. This class triggered the desire to go back to university and complete a degree. Maybe this was really just the paradigm kicking in. But still, you see how one small step, a decision, and easy action gave me a completely new excitement for life. Opportunity was pouring out from the world around me, and so I planned, moved to a new city, and took it.

Around this time, I guess with the new challenges and change of scenarios, I also become more serious and intentional about calmness of mind, focusing on achievement. Meditation raised my expectations, in silence, connecting me with the Supreme Intelligence. It kept me on a reassuring path, feeling peaceful and at ease, taking care of number one. I felt one with my inner voice which kept me strongly in the right order. I was feeling part of the universe with pure creative energy.

Spirit guides you within the Universal Laws, so taking action on intuition is safe and secure, with guaranteed satisfying results both in the short and long term. We become independent and our life starts showing our results, not anyone else's. With reassured confidence, we move forward, making sounder decisions and creating the life we want. Don't stop! Keep focused on your progress. Write it down and carry on.

I also felt I could give back to society. The easiest way was through physical presence in service to the community, so I happily did my part with the recovery fellowship. I gratefully humbled myself so that I could assist other recovering addicts, sharing what I had been given—the means to a new life. Doing so completely banished all self-pity and negative self-talk, opening my eyes to freedom and possibility. Through these opportunities, I realized how blessed I was for having *myself*. I saw the tremendous gift of having a clear mind, enormous health, and my life to use and explore. With those benefits, I could choose how I wanted to live. I was moving toward my *Zen*—a balanced life where I was a channel with a message on being connected and fulfilled.

I couldn't complain anymore. I had no reason not to get on with it. It felt good to help others. I knew I was designed to do more in life, to feel great—if not for others, at least for myself. I wanted to reach my own concepts of success. I wanted to live a meaningful life, in peace, in extasy, actually, one of abundance, easiness, and love. I wanted to exceed my own expectations, to grow on my childhood beliefs of fantastic powers. I wanted to experience life in new and exciting ways, to be able to choose with whom to have dinner or spend that day. Since that young age where I used to sit by the stream of fresh water running in the valley, I felt the calling of the ethereal part of myself, the invisible power of flow. Since that time I have known: I Am.

Each time I needed connection I would go back to that water stream, the rhythm of life through that beautiful soundtrack. You could feel the energy coming and flowing from the earth's center and expanding outward. The expansion was not necessarily good or bad, it was just perfect. A force was trying to talk to me, saying: *Take it, trust me, you have it, it's yours, this pure energy*. Today I know that was life taking over me, choosing me on a leading front of expression; taking over the paradigm and saying, *Believe it*. I'll say it again, I'm that guy who believes in teleportation, time travel, and parallel worlds. I believe thoughts create reality and I believe I deserve all the good things that I desire. The beautiful loving partner, the exotic oceanfront house, the successful career, and the abundance that comes with it all. It's my choice for this timeline!

When I returned to university and moved to the countryside, I felt so in tune with nature that nothing could bother me. I could finally put balance in my energy, or put the *Zen* in my Zenith. *Zen* being the easy energy flow that results from absence of thought; the spirit within. *Zenith* being the acceptance of our greatness. Accepting that I could thrive and peak, change and evolve without restrictions. The two work together to give you all you need, not just to survive. As a growing individual you find your own path, set your own goals, and traverse this unlimited life in a way that doesn't just elevate but also inspires, motivates, and brings us all into our own.

Trust the Expectation Without Questioning

Where do we go from here? We reached a point where we can decide our future and chose the world of tomorrow. We tried many options that brought us here, we have endless options at our fingertips. You just have to flip the switch, turn on the light, accept clarity, and create.

I had dreams when I was a kid … so many dreams! I would climb mountains, write a book, sail the world, make a movie, be an actor, raft down rivers, go skiing in Switzerland, and have a hot tub in the snow. I wanted to drive supercars, jump from an airplane, and be a millionaire with a mansion, have a beautiful wife and happy kids playing outside. I wanted to create a business and a charitable organization, meet royalty, live by the ocean and surf every day. I was full of dreams! Funny, as I write this, I realize that I've accomplished half of this list already. I still need to do the other half! Gosh, I love my life.

I really wanted to change, and I knew that I had to. I realized what I needed to change, and now I knew how to do it. Looking for help, I sought examples. I sought out other successful people who could tell me how they did it, how they turned the tide, how they took over life or what to do to change luck. Each time I'd meet these people, I'd try to extrapolate how they did it. I'd ask them, "What did you do?" Luckily, I met amazing characters always willing to share. Most would have gotten in touch with that inner-self, the gut feeling that in a glimpse—in a fraction of a second—shows you who you really are and that your dreams are a reality. They all agreed: you must give up control of anything else and desire only the things you want to happen. Then, you have to be alert and follow the signs. Follow whenever that nugget of direction shows up. Follow when that intuitive voice tells you, *that's the one,* you grab it, take it, build it in your mind and feel it!

Luckily, the timing couldn't be better than this to envision a new recipe. While you're inspired, claim it, get your signature from the sources of the universe through your creating hand. A decision marks the turning point. It could be hitting rock bottom, having an enlightening experience, or just a moment of awareness and belief. Even if in many cases it helped to shift focus, the turning point doesn't have to be a disaster. Your conscious awareness of it and the desire to create are definitely sufficient.

Once you make the decision, have no doubts about the results. That is the moment you flip the switch and pull back the curtain to show a new scenario of your own making. You see the end result, your desire, and embrace that the path is yours to take. The time is always right, and so it begins. Alan Watts (writer and Zen trainer) said, "You have no obligations to be the same person you were five minutes ago." Now is the right time. While doing this, we're automatically changing our core habits and beliefs. After all, our best knowledge brought us so far, only to find us here. Thus, we need to change from the inside; calming the mind, listening to Spirit, and claiming clarity of thought as we absorb it from the stars and the cosmos. Life changes as soon as we make a decision. Let it flow, through us, manifesting outside us through our conscious thoughts, our intention, and our attitude. This begins a domino effect as we create new results, new circumstances, and, hence, a new life. It doesn't have to be difficult.

I am lucky to have attracted great teachers and examples in my life. While in rehab, I met and followed amazing and successful souls as well as other recovering addicts from different walks of life and various parts of the world. These individuals' success stories resonated in so many ways, as we're all from different backgrounds, with different stories, colors, and shapes. But if we look beyond that, we're just the same, and that was a great lesson for discarding differences and seeing similarities. Spirit, love, souls, and feelings have many methods of expression, but their source is all the same. They're all excellent examples of how it's okay to change you path, your life habits, and your beliefs.

I realized one single truth: I could become whatever I wanted from that day onwards by choosing tomorrow's results. We can start new in each moment. With this realization, a new energy and vibration sparkled inside me. A joy flooded all of the cells of my body, and ideas began to flow. I was now a moving generator of ideas and dreams. I stopped blaming my parents, society, circumstances, or anything else outside of me. I knew that everything that happened to me was a consequence of my previous thoughts and choices. I had received the reflection of my ruling emotional state—my vibrational match. Now, I flipped the switch. It wasn't easy. Hell, it was hard at times, but I did it. And now, with this book, I want to show you how.

My journey was one from that of being an addict to becoming the captain of luxury yachts worth tens of millions of dollars. You will hear tales of the rich and famous, but more importantly, you will hear the stories of those who have found their way. I am one of them, and you can be as well. In astronomy, the Zenith is the high point in the sky directly above the observer. It is the projection of the observer in the cosmic plane. As a noun, Zenith is the time at which something is at its most powerful and successful state. Both descriptions match for me. When you reach the Zenith, you are among the stars.

At this point, we are all observing the sky above, looking to the bright lights and wondering if we will reach them. By the time you finish this book, you will be that light. Those below will be observing your massive ascent. It is within you. It is within us. It is time to shine brightly. Off we go.

Chapter 2

Where Am I?

Where am I? It's a simple question, right? It's not always the easiest one to answer.

As human beings, we often wonder exactly where we stand in this world. Where is our *place*? Is it in the workplace in pursuit of a chosen profession? Is it at home with our children? Is it travelling the world? Is it working to elevate humanity? There are no right answers, only options for you to choose from. As I continue on this wonderful journey, I constantly question my own position in this world. I wonder: *How am I really doing? Am I accomplishing my goals? Am I doing everything I can to pursue my dreams*? Easy questions with easily changing answers.

Listen to Your Inner Voice

How can one evaluate their current position, knowing they might want to be somewhere else? It can be a challenging and frustrating dialogue, as it depends on perspective and the observer. But you have to understand it and let it flow, as it helps to work on yourself in being better than you were yesterday. Like a lighthouse for ships at sea, your inner voice is always a guiding light shining through at all times. There's a reason that phrases like *trust your gut* or *go with your heart* are common. These expressions reference the inner voice that is always inside of you, ready and willing to guide you at all times.

That inner voice that speaks is the person you *really* are, so make the most to listen to listen to it, cherish it, love it, and feel it. It's perfection flowing through you. Grab this guiding force, engage with it, and allow it to help you understand what to do and where to go. You can follow and allow intuition to lead you to great results. Life keeps going in your chosen direction, things keep happening as you want, and you will find yourself feeling better and better. You'll be confident and reassured so you are able to carry on. Nothing is more satisfying than listening to your gut feeling and following as if nothing else matters. Be true to yourself—take on the attitude of *I got this!* You know what you're doing. Your life makes sense; you know you're building it. You're not just blowing in the wind, you're actually creating the wind to support your sails. Following intuition or listening to your inner voice brings the powerful connection with the higher consciousnesses and creating forces of this universe, and that's a beautiful place to be!

I believe intuition and our inner voice are directly from our over-soul or higher self in the universal consciousness realm. Following it is the cleanest and most effective way of staying on your path, as it's within the perfect creation and development of evolution. Its guidance is pure, it has a clean intention, and its clarity allows you to evolve within the fabrics of the universe expressed here on earth. We're operating by the Spiritual Laws, so it can't go wrong. How exciting is it to know the universe has your back? To know that we have in our reach everything that is needed to evolve (and to do it well)? This is why it's so important to make your intuition and inner voice your primary guide; it's the Source talking to you, it will work out.

For years, I didn't listen to my innermost voice. I heard it, but I chose to ignore it thinking I knew better. I went through life without it by my side. It is soul, it is inner being, it is Spirit— it's our true entity, and what you replace it with can be nothing more than a castle made of sand. The replacement will eventually welcome poor choices, fake gods, and self-doubt. The choices I made brought me here today and I'm super grateful. This is why I encourage even young kids to listen to their true self, their signature, their voice, helping them to start early.

Doubt is a terrible guide. It can slow you down creating stuck moments in time that can last forever. All of a sudden you might feel like, *Aaaaaaahhrrggg ... where am I? I was on purpose, doing great, moving forward and completely connected to myself, but now I feel down and out.* Then you find it happened when you allowed doubt to replace your inner knowing. Choose your ruler! It can be the negativity of "flow blocking" doubt, or, the positivity of your confident and intuitive self-loving inner voice. Which one will it be for you? I know which one you want it to be, and that's what we're here for—following joyous intuition!

I will give you an example of my own inner struggle between positive guidance and self-doubt. As I was going full throttle pursuing my dreams, I decided to join university. It was 2002, and I felt as if I needed a degree to succeed in life and move forward. It was the one missing piece. I felt that a degree would make me credible and worthy of a decent future. I needed to acquire this label so that I could be categorized and recognized. People would feel safe and secure when they looked at me, and when they read over my resume. The thought of a degree stating who I was, where I belonged, and what I could do was alluring. At least that was the narrative I told myself, and so, I pursued it. But here I was giving my power away to opinion. Rejecting the voice inside to satisfy my outer circumstances.

We don't need to look to the outside in order to search for a label. Rather, we learn how to look inside and let our inner voice express itself. Let our identity rise, explore it, and express our true natural love. We don't need to be labeled. We are who we are. And even if eventually you get a label, it's one that you are proud of. That's how I felt the system was working at that time and place, I was looking for acceptance. Before I never considered the academic side of it. I didn't see the true benefits it gives, or the knowledge a degree offers. I didn't understand the thought training one experiences at university; the techniques, the teachings, and the endless hours of study. I always believed I was a free spirit and spontaneity would take me where I wanted to go. And it did. But if I wanted something different now, I had to take different actions. *Only a fool makes the same actions and expects different results.* So, I went to university, and I loved it!

Obviously, if you follow what you learned in university, that's a one hundred percent return on your decision to attend. I struggled with feeling as if I couldn't just be me, my true essence, trying my best. It seemed that I was expected to fit nicely into one of the labels that were available in the market so that I could be identified and placed. "Oh, relax! He's a doctor, and she's a dentist." These titles are not who we are; they just tell people what we do! Don't get me wrong. We need the services of doctors and dentists, but there's also a place for other skills and abilities and that place should be explored and not rejected. Thankfully, these days it's easier and more acceptable to be different from the norm. I felt that I needed to explore individual spontaneity, love and fraternity, nature, and letting it be. The thought of sitting in a classroom for endless hours of the day would make me cringe. It just didn't cut it for me, even if I didn't know what I would be when grown up! Still, something told me to sign up, so I did.

I always admired friends and family who knew at a young age what they wanted to do with their professional lives. "I want to be a race car driver," or "I want to be a doctor," or "I want to be an entrepreneur," or "I want to be a lawyer." I daydreamed with all of them. I wanted to be an astronaut! An ocean explorer! A Hollywood actor, or a rock star! I wanted to make millions and live in Monaco and holiday in Mexico. I was a true daydreamer with no need to restrict what I really wanted to do in life; I only knew the end result that I desired! I wanted to live very well and be happy—but I had no idea how to get there. I was simply excited by the possibility and the idea of being it.

To that end, I admired all my friends and family who succeeded through university and became what they wanted to be. They made a choice, stuck to it, and their desire became reality. One-hundred percent success! They had clarity on their position in life and little doubt, only awareness and confidence. I wanted that assurance because I didn't have it at the time.

So I went to school, forging ahead in order to check a box, I didn't really know any better options to move ahead. We can do or be anything we want. We can create our own reality, but we need to study for the challenge, and that was making sense to me. At least that's how I felt at first.

Over time, the rewards began to show up and eventually it was a pleasure. As I changed my perspective and made a decision to make the most of it, my entire focus changed. I was excited, meeting people, studying well, and I had great results. My grades were the best I've ever had. This changed my self-image tremendously. The benefits were great and I felt fantastic. It cleaned my past and refreshed my soul. (Who now knew success tasted like this?) I felt intelligent, smart and knowledge-able. I was having amazing grades in all disciplines, and this was new to me. I felt amazing. I loved it.

I had tried attending university twice, before rehab (while still using drugs), but obviously failed to keep going. I had not been resilient, and instead, I just wanted to get high. My mind wandered when I found classes boring.

On my first attempt, I studied art. C'mon, who fails art? Well, I guess the pot we smoked every day, or the regular acid trips, led me to skip exams. I loved the history—the old artists, the culture, the styles, the ambience, and the who's who of modern art—but I was put off by anything that involved forced creation within narrow limits. You know, the *establishment*, the rules. How can you teach art and impose limits at the same time? Rules and regulations don't work in this setting. Art is the language of emotion and creativity, and those are unlimitedly free. You can learn or teach techniques or secrets of painting and sculpting, but you cannot teach trends. Humans need to label everything around them. Let it be.

Studying art didn't exactly work out for me so the next year I enrolled again. But this time I quit purely because I felt completely out of place. It didn't seem to be adding much to my life. I just couldn't connect with the concept of traveling to school to hear and do things I didn't particularly want to hear or do. It didn't make sense to me to learn, apply, and reinterpret the rules of our ancestors simply because *that's how it is*. I thought, *it doesn't have to be!* Being graded for meaningless projects wasn't for me. After all, why do you need lessons if you're an artist? You just *are* an artist. It was a good try. This was when I had left school yet again and dedicated myself to becoming a full-time drug dealer. This lasted maybe three to four years until I eventually went to rehab and started recovery.

The funny thing is, a few years later while clean and sober and between jobs and courses, I decided to check my artist vein by painting pottery, canvas, and furniture. I did some nice things, mostly out of psychedelic influence due to my past preferences. I wasn't using any drugs, but it was definitely my favorite style, even while sober. I didn't make much money. I gave away most of my favorite pieces. I sold only one of the 30 paintings

I showed, and it was a copy of another masterpiece. That was the day I knew I wasn't a painter and needed to find and follow other direction. I threw all my paintings in the bin, gave my supplies away, and moved on!

On my third attempt at university I was twenty-seven, while most of my fellow students were no more than eighteen years old. On the first day, they thought I was the teacher. Still, I felt like I was eighteen, and I was excited to be at school. I paid attention in classes, did my homework, was on time, and got great grades; mathematics, economics, geography—you name it. I was succeeding in school for the first time in my life. It proved to me that when you want to do something, you will succeed. I hated school before because I felt obliged to attend. But this occasion was different. I *wanted* to learn, and my mood and attitude were both fantastic.

I also felt like this was my last chance. This was my moment to achieve a college degree. I was making sure that I not only passed the exams, but that I also learned the subjects well. My inner voice guided me back to school, and I knew I was in the right place at the right time. And that's what happens following intuition, the inner voice, the gut feeling that no one can hear except ourselves. Only we know what's best for us. If I had asked myself at the time, *where am I?* The answer would have been a resounding, *I am in the perfect place for me!*

While in school, I had to get a part-time job as I had no other source of income. I started working at a call center for roadside and medical assistance. I also decided to move in with my grandmother to save some money. She was alone and I needed a place, so we joined forces. It was great, I had a fantastic time and she was always there for me; she was a great source of advice in many subjects. I could tell that I was also a source of happiness for her, too, so we made it work for a few years.

I was working in the morning, studying at night, and just getting by. Things were really working out. I was working towards something. I had a goal to graduate and make loads of money to support a great lifestyle. I had a refreshed vision that life does get better. I believed I was going to be a better person with a better life. I had new hope for my future self—successful, rich, and I would travel the world.

I wanted to experience new things. I wanted to live more, buy my own house, live well, and find my beautiful, loving, and caring wife. I knew that if I focused and worked for it with patience and calmness, I would have a chance at these goals. All our wishes come true if we really desire them and put our energy into it.

Have you ever felt that way? As if your life is in perfect harmony and heading in the absolute correct direction? You have no doubts, only direction and confidence. It is a wonderful feeling because you can focus on the simple challenges in front of you, resolute in your purpose so you are not creating additional obstacles.

Things were going well, but not all was perfect as I had some issues with the law in the form of two court cases. One was a paternity claim from a lesbian couple; I had a strange afternoon surrounded by cocaine, ecstasy pills and oblivion, had sex with one of the women and never saw her again until the child was one year old. They had a plan. They just wanted to be independent mums and I wasn't supposed to ever find out, but it didn't turn that way, as nine months later the police came after me. Oh well ... the 90's! The other court case was just before checking into rehab, I lost a car in an auto-accident. I had to fly out of town the next morning, so I couldn't defend myself in the case. The accident had occurred early in the morning, and, thankfully, I wasn't overly intoxicated (otherwise, I'd be in a tough situation). Basically, the authorities were all over me to pay bills, answer in court, and they wouldn't leave me alone. I had nothing to pay them with, but they wouldn't accept that as an excuse. With this twist, my perspective on life changed again, and suddenly the air was a bit too heavy to be sober, but I kept clean. This period was one of the darkest moments in my recovery.

I stayed sober, went to meetings, did my service, helped others, worked part-time, and went to school. I kept my head down and my purpose high. I was trying with all I had to fit in, to gain acceptance, and to thrive. But I remember the constant feeling of being overwhelmed. I kept asking the universe: *For fuck's sake! Give me a break now, will you?* But, in truth, I had to be the one to make a difference. Through this extraordinarily challenging time, I relied heavily on my inner voice to guide me through thick and thin. In fact, that is the great beauty of having a strong guiding force; it stays with you at all times, and it doesn't run and hide.

I was close to a breakdown, with no help from *Dr. Feel Good*. No beers, no dust, no pills—no drugs at all. I had to deal with this straight up and clean. Meditation was all I had as I juggled everything I could, kept my eye on the ball, and asked for help and advice when needed. The funny part is, adversity shows you how much you can actually stretch yourself. Your perceived limits aren't actually your real ones.

A Painful Wakeup Call

Then, something happened. From my deepest sorrow and pain came the biggest lesson of my life. When in recovery, one of the 12 steps of the program requires you to create a list of all the people you have harmed. Next, you must make amends to them all, if and when appropriate. Some apologies require more time and effort than others. At this time, I was trying to regain acceptance from one side of my family. I was trying to be allowed back home again. Not to move in, but just to visit, hug, enjoy meals, and laugh. I wanted to reconnect. After all, this was the house I grew up in since I was born. It was home and I wanted back in. I had the idea I could go back in time and pick up the seven-year-old kid who I was before it started to go sideways, believing I could erase all the bad shit. I was advised by my counselor not to. He said, "Let it go, don't do it. You've been there, things happened. You were kicked out, asked not to come back, so don't do it. Wish them well, and let it go."

But in my stubbornness, I wanted the recognition of my new well-being—the new version of myself, the new person, clean, sober and reliable. I wanted them to accept my apologies. I was forcing and demanding recognition. That's not how it works. We have to follow the path of least resistance, state our intentions, and let it go, let the universe take care of the rest. This brings me the Universal Law of Forgiveness: *We must learn to accept our own mistakes and let go of them completely. We must forgive ourselves before we forgive others. Forgiveness empowers and heals the one who forgives, allowing Love to flow either way.* I was trying too hard to erase my past mistakes when I realized it was not possible. I had been through it. I've apologized and made amends, so now it was time to let go and face a new life. All I had to do was to forgive myself.

As you can imagine, both my parents had expelled me from their lives, unwilling to deal with a junkie. I didn't blame them. I only wanted to recreate a sense of family and repair the damage I had done. I wanted to find the love in the roots, and I wanted it now. I was following my ego instead of my inner voice. My inner voice was telling me: *forget it, leave it, move on, accept and be happy, you're not a junkie anymore!*

I was working to be forgiven and I didn't quit. I kept doing everything I could to gain forgiveness and approval, hoping my family might accept the new me. They didn't owe me anything; I was just wanting it to happen. I guess it was important to me. It probably was the ego searching for its recognition (it most certainly was), even if backed up by good intention. I couldn't demand it, and I couldn't control it. It would have to be a gift from the kindness of their hearts, or it wouldn't be at all. I forgave myself and I forgave them, so it was not my business anymore. Still, as a stubborn kid, I was trying to build the relationship with my father and working to repair the damage. I was trying too hard as he still didn't want to see me or even have me around his house, let alone inside. And maybe that was the right thing. Maybe we had our experience and that was it. Maybe. But something inside was making me come back and try again. I would knock on the door, I would ring the bell, I would try to meet for lunch or a chat, and usually I would get an excuse to why it couldn't work out. Then the day came when I decided to call and wish him a happy birthday. On this day, I got the strongest wake-up call I've ever had.

At the time, my dad had a yacht, and he would spend long periods of time on holiday with his new family. He answered the phone; "Oh, it's you. Thank you, we are all together here on the yacht celebrating with your brothers, sisters, and cousins." The entire family united except me. I was devastated, speechless, looking into space when he carries on, "We are all here together. Bye now." And hangs up the phone.

I couldn't believe what just happened, and in anger, I let the phone drop from my hands. I had never felt so bad in my entire existence, and I asked, *why?* I felt the deepest sorrow. The old familiar pain of rejection had come back and hit me with its hardest punch. I felt empty, null, stupid, worthless, and dealing with these emotions in a sober state made things more difficult. A large group of my loved ones were celebrating together, and no one told me a thing about it or even tried to include me. It hurt like hell. I cried. I couldn't hold it, I was sobbing like a child. I had been in recovery for four years, doing what I was told: humbling myself, following direction without questioning, ignoring my desires to satisfy others—and this is what I got? I quickly realized they hadn't forgiven or forgotten the pain I had caused. And not only that, they had no plans to see me. I felt rejected again and couldn't quite believe this was happening. I felt it in every cell of my body.

In that moment, I felt like I wanted to throw in the towel. The feeling of rejection was not new to me, however. Easing the pain of rejection is why I began using drugs in the first place. There had always been a huge anger and rejection in my direction, and I never knew why. And now, years later, I was hit anew by this old, familiar sting. I didn't expect it. Not now, not again, not sober!

I had enough. I was anguished and sad on a level I had never experienced before. I literally wanted to die. I wished to die in that moment when the phone fell from my hand to the ground. *It's pointless to live like this*, I thought. Nothing seemed worse than working hard to gain the approval of others only to be rejected again. I felt anger, sadness, and every negative emotion there was to experience. *To live for this ... I might as well be dead*, I thought. I saw the pattern that carried me all those years. I saw where it was coming from, my addiction, the accidents, overdoses, and car crashes. But I didn't know why or from where this rejection was coming. I was devastated, and I wanted to die.

Recovery was all about self-esteem, getting well, and getting back on track. It was about making amends with family. I had clearly failed. Well, I didn't *fail* because I was still drug free, I was happy at university, and I was becoming a respectable member in society. But now, I was in a miserable state. I was expecting others to change while I changed, but that didn't happen. However, I couldn't see it that way. All I could feel was my old companion, rejection. I felt pushed away, like an undesirable, useless mistake. The clear voice of my counselor popped into my head: *Don't do it, don't go there, leave it, accept and let go*, which proved I didn't see what was really around. What else was I wrong about? It was a strange moment.

I told myself I was at fault for even being alive. I cried for days; at work, in school, in the car, anywhere I felt depression hit me. Ten days go by in this miserable state, feeling lost and unwanted—I was feeling like shit. Barely eating, overcaffeinated, smoking too much, and not speaking with anyone. There was nothing except for that feeling of, "What am I doing here?" And then, three weeks after that phone call, I had a massive heart attack. My heart stopped, and I fell to the ground. Eyes open, understanding everything that was happening.

I had felt a bit funny during the previous week, with a strange sensation in my body and Spirit. My entire aura was fuzzy and cloudy, like a dirty martini. This was unusual, not being fully in charge of myself, or present and aware of my surroundings. I had constant uncertainty, a lack of clarity. I didn't know why, but I was low on energy, distracted, disconnected, numbed by the sadness of recent events. Sometimes, I would just cry like a baby, in so much pain while driving back and forth between school and work. It was as if I was under some kind of anesthesia, under a dark cloud. I wasn't my full self. I felt as if I had been hit by a train and had to carry on. Those days, my mood was heavy, running low on energy with a general *I don't care* vibe, but I didn't see this coming. I never thought I'd have a health issue like this. I never thought it could happen to me.

Adversity has a way of knocking you off, leaving you to ponder, *what the hell just happened?* You then stray further from your morals, ambitions, and guiding light. In those moments, you are most susceptible to tragedy. I have found that when you put your guard down, you leave yourself open to all that life can hit you with. In reality, you need your guiding light the most when you experience the greatest amount of adversity.

Hit with a Heart Attack

The afternoon of my heart attack, my cousins and I were having fun riding our dirt bikes on a racetrack behind the house at my grandmother's place. I had been living there for two or three years at that point, and we were a good team. The house was within walking distance from at least eight other houses belonging to cousins. My great grandmother and her husband, whom I never met, bought this beautiful 200-year-old stone house on a big farm. After a large fire, it had been literally rebuilt to spend the winters with the help of their eleven sons. In those days, it was normal to have so many children. And all of those children eventually had between five and seven children of their own, who then each had between three to five children themselves. Needless to say, we are a very big family. Consequentially, with changing times the land on the main farm was slowly divided between siblings and generations, creating smaller country houses where all the neighbors are first, second, or third generations of family members with vineyards, cork oak, cedars, stone pine, and olive trees between acres and acres of forest! It was amazing.

I grew up very close to many of my cousins. Even my father's house was close by (where I lived growing up), touching borders with the main farm since they bought the property when he married my mother. Being a farm, one of the main activities besides hiking, picking fruit, planting trees, and horse-riding was riding dirt bikes. With time, we made a track. That day, we were riding around on the vineyard track dusting one another and enjoying the late summer sun. It was September 14, 2004. It was a slow day. I was taking it easy on my dirt bike, and at some point, I felt sick, misplaced, a bit hazy and tired . As I made my way to the house, I could feel that something was not right. I was dizzy and riddled with pain, with a sensation of pins-and-needles. It was difficult to breathe like there was a knot on my throat and I knew I had to get home. I waved goodbye to my cousins and made my way back.

As I made it to the garage a mile away, I got off the bike to open the gate and push the bike inside. As I turned around, I felt even dizzier and my head was spinning. As I approached the shed, my heart hurt like hell and my body literally switched off. I fell flat like a tree. *Boom!* Face down, nose first. I could see the ground coming closer, but I couldn't do anything to stop it. *Pow!* Straight and direct onto the ground I fell. I remember thinking, *this should hurt my nose, but why can't I feel a thing?* I hadn't been breathing regularly since I left my cousins to return home. I sucked in air hard, took a big breath and tried to get up, but immediately fell down again face first. *Bam.* The pain in my chest was so strong that I couldn't feel anything else.

On the floor, I had another perspective on the situation as I couldn't move a finger or even blink. I waited a bit, analyzing this confusing symptom that was all new to me. After some time, thought to myself: *Hmmmm ... I must have fainted or have low blood pressure. I'll get up now.* I took another breath and got myself upright again. I was pale with cold sweat, there was tremendous pain in my chest, and I gasped for air as I pushed the bike inside. I closed the gate, hoping this was only indigestion.

I leaned on the gate, almost leaning down to my knees, and turned around. Meanwhile, I'm thinking: *Gosh, I'm still in pain, still dizzy, this is a terrible state. I guess I'll make it home.* I barely took three steps before I fell flat again. This time, I felt an even more intense pain in my chest, arm, and leg, and I literally couldn't breathe. There was no air coming in. I fell down on my face, and this time, I knew it was for good. I couldn't move. I had no juice running through me and I could feel my body in shut-down mode. Nothing was happening except this voice, this inner being, this conscious awareness of what was happening. I was on the ground, static, with no breath and a pain that I could never describe, yet, I was still consciously thinking: *what the hell is going on with me?*

Time slowed down. I could hear crickets, and I could feel a fly which had landed on my nose. I could see the road, the sand on my face, and the trees. Everything was present, alive, it all had more current than me; there was energy everywhere. I could feel the Earth's energy as a whole, spinning, I could see it flowing in the trees. The earth was alive. The wind, the birds and leaves—everything around me was alive, colors, sounds, even the air. There was a moment of acknowledgement that I wasn't breathing. For the first time, I saw and felt the consciousness of a tree, of the entire earth, and in the present moment, I acknowledged: *ah, there you are, on the floor.*

It felt like an elephant was sitting on my chest. I panicked, thinking: *something is really wrong with me.* In my mind, I was fighting to get up and move but yet I had no physical reaction, not even a blink. I couldn't move my eyes, yet I could see everything and more. Nothing was working. All systems were down except my new vision, my hearing, my awareness of the surroundings; my essence, my *Being* was alive, and I had exceptionally clear consciousness. It was so strange. Time and space merged into one bubble of motion, sound, and color of a new density. I could see and hear the life happening around me. I could understand the clouds and feel the *now* like never before—but yet, I could not move.

It became a spiritual experience. I felt closer to the wind than I did to my own body. I was aware of my surroundings, I could feel energy, but with my body, nothing was going on. Stillness. The mind was clear and present. This was the strongest pain I'd ever felt, and I don't wish it on anyone. It was right in the heart, the love center of our body. It was like my soul was being extracted from my heart. Every thirty seconds or so I managed to grasp for a tiny bit of air. Was I dead? My body felt dead, but I was wide awake, analyzing and thinking. I did not understand what was going on.

I was lucid and giving orders to my brain: *get up and walk, turn around, breathe now, breathe,* but there was no response. My body wasn't listening. It was not obeying the usual commands. *I'm dying,* I thought. This is how it feels to be dying! This is it! I changed my perception. I switched from panic to analyzing. What is going on with me? This is it, the end! I can't move. I can't breathe. My body doesn't work. Shit, I must be dying.

I couldn't believe it. I had flashback after flashback to my life, and to the people I loved and wanted to see again. I hadn't accomplished much of anything yet; I was trying, but was still so far from my desires. I didn't want to die. As much as I had struggled lately or thought that my life was uninteresting, I still didn't want to die. I could feel the tears rolling down my cheek and I was overcome by a huge sense of sadness. It was heartbreaking to say goodbye to life.

That's when I realized how much I loved life and wanted to be here, alive. With so much more to do, so much beauty to see and experience, I realized I had taken for granted all the small things that make up our days: walking in the park, loving, swimming, laughing, or just breathing, for God's sake! In this moment of sadness, I felt the most honest feeling toward our planet I had ever experienced: *Oh fuck ... I'm dying, and I don't want to. How did I get here? All those plans, all those ideas and desires, all those things to do, so much to say, so much more life ahead, why? Who's in charge? I don't want to die.*

This was a turning point in my awareness of the world and my role In it. I could see it all now—the physical world, the mental or thought world, the ether, the floating consciousness that links it all together. I could see and feel this great energy of nothingness that keeps us stuck and makes us give up on our dreams by destroying our ambition. We end up not believing in ourselves, afraid of actually living our best timelines. But we can break the barrier in the here and now, in the present. In this moment, I learned that nothing is more valuable than my life and the drive to make the most of it. I could see the veil separating the *on/off* sides of our current reality; I could see the easiness and fragility of what actually being alive is all about. We take it for granted and it's so easily taken like this. Although impressed with my new revelations, I was mostly sad that my physical experience of life was coming to an end. This was a new dimension for me. I had found a spiritual world behind the curtain. I was having a spiritual view of this reality.

Where am I? I kept asking, wondering, thinking, and repeating it. *Where am I?* Fully conscious and aware, but with a heavy body, heavy heart (in pain), and no oxygen. The obvious answer was that I was physically incapacitated, on the ground, and likely dying. But as I dove deeper, I realized that I was just lost in the moment with a strange feeling that everything was there, present, connected. *Where am I?* I allowed my heartache to drive me to a deep, dark place. It didn't have to be that way, but I brought it into me. The writing was on the wall. Why? Because I lost direction and stopped letting intuition guide me. When a boat stops using the guiding light from a lighthouse, it is most susceptible to striking land.

Then a funny thing happened. As I was lying on the ground, I saw two cousins driving by on their motorcycles. They were just fifty meters away and I knew they could not see me. As I struggled, I heard the sound of their engines, but I couldn't lift my hand or shout to get their attention. I just saw them out of the corner of my eye. I'm thinking: *They can't see me. Shit ... there goes my chance to be rescued! How am I getting out of here?* In a dark sense of humor, I can laugh about it now! They drove by and I was alone again, thinking: *Fuck! There goes my chance!*

I was working through my thoughts when I was interrupted by even more excruciating pain. It was so hard, so painful, right in my chest. I couldn't gasp for more air and I didn't have air in my lungs to breathe anymore, let alone air to scream for help. That was it, no more I felt. I remember looking to the side as I felt that I was being pulled underground. I saw a bunch of hands emerging from the ground, through the dirt, grabbing me and pulling me down to the earth, respecting the cycle. I mentally fought, not wanting to go six feet under. I stayed flat on the dirt floor as I mentally fought, trying to get up. I couldn't move. My body was still not obeying the will of my mind's desire. I had no air, no fuel, and my body couldn't work without it. I knew it. So, with great sadness, I decided to quit fighting. I said to myself: *Fine ... so be it. That's it. It's time... Let's go to the next step.*

One minute. That's all it took for me to feel the coldness of the end, to recognize my life would be no more. That was it, my day of reckoning had unexpectedly come. All I could think to myself was: *where am I?* It is an easy question to ask but a challenging one to answer honestly. The Spirit World was revealing itself and I could safely feel it. I was in a *dimension* where I could see and feel Life Energy everywhere around me; on stones, sand, trees, and the wind. I could understand the physics of our world. This is when I started dissociating from my body. I was partly in a different dimension and partly still in the physical world. That was intriguing. I got curious with that side of the experience, *Where am I? What have I done to get here?*

To that point I would ask, where are you? Are you happy in your life? Content? Satisfied? Do you have dreams? I bet you might feel as if there is still work to be done. You aren't complete, you're not quite there. That is correct, as we all have work to do. But check in. Know who you are, where you are, and where you want to be. Those are important definers within your path, within your existence. Your inner voice can be the lighthouse that guides you through choppy waters and safely to harbor. Use it as you can. It is always present and there for the taking.

I let go and stopped fighting for my life. I quit. I had to let go and accept defeat. The pain was so excruciating, it was not worth holding on to. Whatever happened at that point was stronger than my will to survive. Letting go was the only option, and, because I had just experienced it, I knew there was still something else after. I had a glimpse of this other side, this dimension where life was still happening, but in a very different way, a different density. I was fearless and curious, nonetheless. So, I let go, wondering what would come next.

I had thought earlier that all would be well if I could just get up and see a doctor. But no. With my back flat on the ground, looking up to the sky. I was conscious of my transition. I would soon be available to the vultures. This would be the end. *C'est la vie, world*

Chapter 3

Ascending

*We never really die. We ascend, connect with the
Source, and remember who we are.*

The most extraordinary sequence came next. As I released
my physical body, my consciousness—my soul, my inner
being, me a Spirit—lifted off the ground, abandoning
the physical body. I realized I was no longer fighting or holding
onto life, I Am Life! I only was holding onto the physical part of
my life, the body! I was still alive. I was well! I separated from
my physical form and fluidly moved away, easily, just as soon as
I let it, like water running through a net. It was a disassociation
of sorts, but one I could clearly feel and see. As I moved away
from my physical body, I didn't feel pain anymore. Instead, I felt
alive! It was the best sensation ever of purity and perfection, a
place where everything *Is*, clear and vibrant. I was so impressed.

The pain was gone, and I was bliss. The realization, "I am Spirit, not the body." I am whole, pure joy, loving. While the body feels pain, the Spirit only feels the energy of flowing life.

Things started clearing up. Leaving the body was more of a relief than anything else. I felt free, felt plenitude, high-vibration energy, and well-being flowing through me. I never felt so well in my life before, and I had tried many things. This vibration was the best I ever had. Not only I am flowing with bright white light and purple and bluish tones of energy, but I *am* the energy. Like an endless source of flourishing life. I realized this floating to the sky, leaving my body behind and naturally just *being*. I was a ghost, looking down on my motionless body in a loving way accepting my fate but curious to follow through. Life is really full of surprises beyond your comfort zone.

This was a moment of great insight on existence, and into the perfect Spirit inside of me and you. I now clearly knew that *I am* Spirit. The body is just a vehicle for our soul's personal development. Yes, I'd read about it and heard people talk about it, but this time, I had experienced it firsthand. Everything is much different when you experience it for yourself. You can hear stories until the end, but a firsthand dance with this theory of the body and Spirit is unlike anything else. And now I could see it. I felt it and knew it. It's pure love. It's blissful. It's perfection. It's knowledge. It's plenitude. It's energy. We are energy. The earth, the trees, the bugs, the water, the oceans and skies, I can see it all. We're all connected, dancing to different tones but all an expression of the same creative force, different manifestations of intention, of Life Source. I stay in this moment for a while, being it.

I have it, and it feels fantastic. It vibrates and I can easily and instantly move through space with no friction at all. I easily connect with the empirical knowledge available in this non-physical state of being. This happens as I continued ascending from my body and into heaven.

I experienced a strange, invisible sense of respect and obedience to this evolving energy; this unlimited feeling of power mixed with an absolute feeling of belonging. Somehow, I felt back at home. I understood how everything is alive and shares the same energy. In receiving this valuable lesson, I gained a different respect for the trees, the bugs, and even for the stones. They are not just objects; rather, they are energy, consciousness just like us. They're an expression of the same Supreme Intelligence, consciously seeking evolution and function, aligned in a different vibration that gives them a different purpose. To extinguish their energy is to affect our own, as we all are connected to each other. It's all that is.

As I kept moving up, away from the physical, ascending, I was feeling better and better. I saw my energy field with a wider range, with new functions, abilities, and perceptions. We are much more, and much more is around and above us. We just need to acknowledge and connect to it. I kept going up, floating faster, higher and being pulled in one direction even if I feel that I could reach anywhere in space with no limits. At one point, I looked down, only to see my physical body lying there flat on the ground. It was static and frozen. I wasn't worried about it, I understood I was now on a new level. However, I was intrigued. I marveled. *So, this is how it happens. This is how we go, and how we move on. This is death.* With this realization, I lost all fear of dying and of death. We never die, we simply change form and dimension. Consciousness keeps running, joyous, growing, expanding, and learning. We keep *being*. Life is eternal.

It didn't hurt anymore. Without pain, I felt wonderful and light. As I ascended, I took in masses of information. Flying through the air, I learned a great deal about myself, about life, and, of course, about the afterlife. Physical death is not final. It's like a curtain that drops in the theater, and a new scene begins, except for the body, which remained on the ground. That body needed this energy and vibration to make its heartbeat. It will be awkward when someone finds its lifeless form. There should be a sign for the ones that stay and find the body: *Don't worry, be happy; they are well in the afterlife, let them go!*

It might be sad for a few or upsetting to many to find a dead body, unresponsive, cold, and heavy. But that's just part of the human experience. Occasionally, the excitement would hit me again that life is a Spirit that never dies. It just travels, evolves, changing bodies, form and dimensions. It is fucking cool what we are, and where we come from. I knew I was moving on to another chapter.

A New Beginning

This was not the end, but rather, a new beginning. I felt more alive than ever before. I was impressed to finally realize the truths that I only suspected before. I had wondered what it might feel like when we depart. Would I retain all the knowledge I learned in my time on earth? Or, would I be a blank canvas, navigating the world in my brand new shiny body? Only time would tell, but one thing I immediately understood, to each its own—what happens in the physical world belongs there. Knowledge, thought, and consciousness can shift dimensions, but the concerns are totally different. Most of our worries really don't matter at all, except on earth while in physical form, and even here, they shouldn't bother us!

As I was coming up, through the blue sky, things got extremely dark—nearly pitch black. For a good while I couldn't see a thing. Then I noticed a small light in the distance. It was the exit light at the end of a long tunnel. I was rapidly moving toward it. Then, *bam*, I was there. I join the light and keep ascending, slower now, still feeling blissful. I was relaxed but intrigued with what would come next. This was all new, coming to terms with death, or, coming to terms with life after death, I should say.

I guess I was very surprised as it seemed like an endless journey with no destination as I kept just going. I was well with it. I accepted it as it came, effortlessly voyaging through the air while feeling extremely well, so why not. I happily trusted this new experience, because if that was dying, it wasn't bad at all. It was great! I was excited and surrendered at the same time. There I was, just consciousness and me. This experience was so clear, so lucid; it was as real to me as typing this text or as real as you are reading it. This is living the afterlife in person. It was so enriching, so gratifying, to be given the opportunity to go through this experience.

It was incredible, I was *living* an experience I used to think of as mere fantasy. It changed my entire understanding of life and of our abilities. I laughed at the thought of trying to explain something like this to my friends or family. But then again, would

I now even have the same family? Would I find a new vessel with a new life and new beings in it? Was I going to reincarnate? Right now? Later? Would I become a green fellow in a yellow lake on a green planet? I happily kept moving, feeling the safety of perfection in this new form. Somehow, I knew it was good and answers would come soon. I felt it.

Flying through the clouds as condensed energy I began to level out, moving horizontally and eventually reaching an area just above the clouds of different energy—or let's say, in different densities. A plateau made of the same substance. A bright bluish white color with good vibration. I realized we're the same, just condensed differently, like unique mixtures of the same content, hanging out in a sea of energy with an amazing feeling of plenitude and easiness.

I was relaxed with mixed feelings, though still a bit sad I had left everyone without saying goodbye. Yet, I was excited to be here, experiencing, finding out what's next: afterlife. I didn't want to die, but I was also very surprised and excited that *I didn't* die. Right now I *am* this experience. This was the best feeling ever, such a high vibration, such abundance and bliss. I felt more alive than ever, which was ironic because my body wasn't looking so hot. As they say, we only value what we have once it's gone.

As I was beginning to enjoy the excitement and truly marinate in all that was happening, I received massive amounts of information on everything that was happening around me. By induction, telepathy, absorbing from that which I was now part of, I understood where I was going and what I was doing. As much as I was surprised by the unknown, I was also aware of what was happening. A knowing, like a reminder, as if I was receiving answers immediately as I asked the questions, with no hesitation, no downtime, or confusion, only answers collated to questions flying all around me at every moment.

My mind alternated between *what is going on here?* and *oh, yes, I'm a free Spirit flying out of my body, heading into space, cool!* Since leaving my physical body, I experienced only the best parts of existence; there was no luggage to carry, no stomach to feed, no lungs that required air, there was no weight resistance to movement, no intellectual restrictions or any other type of opposition. Freedom takes its true meaning in this form. It was a constantly reassured state of new beginning, a positive beginning; magical, unlimited, unrestricted, and uncensored, and I could only be excited about it. I felt as if I was being shown the full potential of our existence, or at least some of the ways we can go about it. I understood our origins, our existence. I am now, in fact, a flying body of energy.

How assuring to realize that only good things happen to us! So, yes, I did believe I was in a good place, a good system, a good era, and a good direction. I was feeling well and all-knowing, vibrating in peace, being it. This is me and I know it. Surrounded by light energy, easiness, in a positive sequence of events, with a magical sense of perfection, understanding, and peace—that was pure heaven. It is an easy and effortless way of being alive, with no suffering, no pain, just light, plenitude, clarity, and flow. And, interestingly (did I mention?), no need for food or air to breathe, no need for clothes, cars or airplanes! And the beautiful thing is, everyone around you is feeling the same way; you know it and they know it, so no one is trying to take it from you and you're not trying to take it from anyone else. We all have it; it's everywhere, and there is a lot of it. It is all that is. We are *it*.

I became relaxed in this new-found understanding and aware-ness of the peace and tranquility that ruled existence. I saw the larger picture of how we belong to something bigger—way bigger. I suddenly felt connected to space, to the earth, to the stars, to the universe, and to an immense source of knowledge far beyond anything else I'd ever seen or felt. It all confirmed another suspicion; through the years and civilizations, we received a lot of distorted information here on earth.

The majority of the population's way of living is wrong. We waste life and squander our abilities away. They (the higher Spirits) know that we can do better and be better, elevating our-selves to their vibration by using our innate abilities to focus on the best version of ourselves. Letting go, accepting, expressing love. Evolving, providing the Spirit within the best experiences on earth, as it's the will of the Supreme Intelligence. If we're the tip of the iceberg, we are part of the same; we are part of an immense system of living with many different dimensions and planes of expression. If we are in a system that allows us to physically be here, the least we can do is to use our abilities to be our best selves. Firstly, we should be very happy that we're given the opportunity to come here every day and play, expand, evolve, grow, and to choose and create as an extension of the source. Thank you. We must be grateful, not only for us to make the most of our time on earth (and this can benefit every-one around and above us), but also for our origin to evolve from our experiences. We are connected to our origins. If we make life on earth better, we'll be benefitting the whole. The whole grows as we grow. If we acknowledge our origins, our *powers*, and with this acknowledgement, elevate ourselves to the powerful beings we are capable of becoming, we change not only the way of life here on the earth, but also above, in the universe. We make a positive difference. We are here, on earth, but still connected to our origins, the universal consciousness which speaks and listens to us instantaneously at all times. It learns and benefits from our growth. Imagine we're in a lab, evolving and developing life experiences, and universal consciousness is learning the results of what we do. Not judging, but learning! Shouldn't we at least try to be our best selves? I guess we must!

We are programmed for this deep inside our hearts and souls. We know it. The thing is, not only do we get easily distracted by commercial agendas, but also, we're taught in school to ignore it. So only a few people act or reflect upon this, giving it life, will, and direction. Rather, the majority continue heading in a chosen direction with no bigger goals than watching the football game, getting drunk in the pub, believing in politicians, or focusing on material possessions. I like material possessions. I want a Ferrari, I love to sail, and I love watching the Grand Prix! These things excite me. Through the development of this last decades, a new age is here, where major discoveries and schools are being directed in these subject areas, learning and exploring the teachings of the nonphysical, allowing it to flow through. This development is phenomenal and very gratifying, hence me finally writing this book after seventeen years! Today, there is an evolving class devoted to this side of humanity and it's fantastic to be part of it.

Please be aware that I admire all men and women who are dedicated to an activity, sport, or scholarship, those who are specialists in any area. Teachers, engineers, historians, any passionate dedicated people—it's inspiring and it's within our purpose to evolve our species. I have goals for myself. I get up and chase my dreams, and that's a wish I have for everyone on this planet. Fortunately, there are as many expressions of life on earth. These expressions produce brilliant scientists, mathematicians, philosophers, or carpenters, all of whom keep us evolving into great comfort. As important are the camper, the hippie, and the homeless, they are all a contribution to life experience, contrast and knowledge. It's part of the duality of this planet. This life on earth can be much more than what we're told. We can do more and have a much higher quality of life. This is for us to explore and better understand. It took me dying to actually understand how to live.

Millions of fantastic ways of respecting life and valuing higher principles are available to us. I only learned those lessons when I became aware that I'm part of the energy. It was literally a fantastic out-of-body experience, one I will never forget. Life didn't seem complicated anymore, partly because I was no longer thinking it—I was *being* it. Life is easy, I could see that when I was no longer living it by the *mind*.

The mind can save us or enslave us. From Spirit, life is easy and beautiful. Death, as I saw it, was to be trusted, enjoyed, and even celebrated. However, I was likely alone in that sentiment. While I was flying through the air, thrilled in nothing more than energy and consciousness, my loved ones below were about to learn of my demise.

For the masses, though, when someone dies or leaves this form of manifestation, it is normal to be sad and overly emotional. Don't get me wrong, I get sad as well. Recently, I lost two uncles at once, so I understand. It's sad. But then, I realize how much fun they're having and how much they are enjoying their new discoveries! I remember why I loved them! Some people get angry and dwell on the loss for long periods of time. We don't like losing who we love, even if it is to a higher level. We like talking with them; we like their company, their essence. However, it is not the end. It's just a change in the level of activity. They are not dead. Rather, they have transitioned, released their physical body. We should not only be happy for them that they made it, but also be grateful for what they're doing out there, behind the veil, accomplishing and living with bigger tasks to perform. Or let's say, they're backstage, on a different dimension of being.

Thus, the sadness related to death is less about the one who dies and more about those who remain behind. They miss the person, selfishly, wishing for more time. But I know firsthand that those who are gone are not actually gone. They are now detached from the physical world and getting on with their new existence. Living. As I ascended up and through the air, I understood that death is not to be feared. It just *is*. A change in form and set. It will come for each of us, but will not act as an end. It will usher us into a new form of existence, one where we can form new memories, experiences, and relationships. Plus, we get to reincarnate! How exciting is that? Who knows, maybe you will eventually come again to play a new chosen role on earth, with a new family, in a new age! Developing and evolving your personality with new ideas and a new mission or message to deliver, you'll complete the cycle of consciousness and physical body together again. You probably won't have any memories from your previous life experiences; however, you'll be comfortable with it because you'll have the knowledge that those experiences provided to you. I guess reincarnation could be another book by itself!

It's hard to believe, but I was dead in the physical world. Three times I was gone; this first, by myself in front of the garage, and twice again later in the hands of family and medical staff, as I'll explain shortly. If only my loved ones could have understood that I was okay each time, while on the other side, in the afterlife. I was in love as I transitioned to the new stage, but I could not communicate with those around me. They'd have to experience it for themselves one day, when they'd realize they hadn't reached the end, but rather, a new beginning. But as quickly as things change, they can often change again. That's what happened to me in another surprising and unexpected turn of events.

Chapter 4

Connection

*Meeting my Spirit Guides, getting a life review, and
the extension of my Soul.*

On the bluish white space of the clouds and in the vibrating energy, I was curiously waiting, contemplating and soaking in the feeling complete, although bodiless no space, no time moment. A state of plenitude, standing calm and peaceful. Within seconds, another energy entity similar to myself with a different vibration but alike in composition shows up. This being was definitely more comfortable than myself in this environment. He was familiar with this atmosphere and this form of being, and he had a very strong, huge presence, vibrating and sending off a bright light; an excellent energy. Emanating a vibe of perfection and knowledge, serene, projecting a grandiose purpose full of meaning. He knew of his importance yet humble about his position in the great hierarchy of things as I could feel his connection with something bigger. With an elegant posture, a representation of the Supreme Intelligence, he promptly projected information with truth and clarity.

Though at first intimidated, I soon found trust. His presence was powerful but peaceful, and I could feel he answered to something far more powerful than either of us. I knew I was in the presence of a Supreme Entity and shortly understood by his attitude that there's a lot more above and around us than what we see, what we know, what we are told, or what we want to know.

I was experiencing a unique and humble moment of clarity, and the range of awareness in that moment revealed the tremendous ability of our mind's hidden capacities. The links are phenomenal as you feel the connection and networking among different energies, substances, and dimensions. You've always had these capacities, but they were temporarily forgotten or simply unused. You can feel the energy that connects these bodies of knowledge, as it's the same energy that encompasses everything else. You feel the constant vibration; you feel life. You feel the creative systems, the creative power, the easiness of creation, the power of thought and its relation to this energy-forming matter. This was when I realized how easy life could be. I thought: *If I get to choose to go back to Earth again, I'll choose to already be rich and have a successful life.* This is where you see how thoughts and choices create reality, how the fabric is made, how it is powerfully connected, and how literally we choose who and what we are.

You see how one thought can easily move the energy to create. You see how the planet is alive with the same creative, pure, and perfect force that is in us. You see how we are part of this in a structural and creative way, and it's almost inexplicable how incredible it feels. The physics of a perfect living system were present and exposed from their core to the atmosphere and beyond. You understand how we can only know perfection if we follow the nature of this system.

In this setting I could see the laws of physics operating everywhere. I understood and felt laws I've never studied before. I recognized the truth of this system. I met a Spirit with a different purpose than my own, or the missions we have been pursuing in our physical bodies on earth. It was an amazing and fantastic experience, to say the least. I felt blessed.

He acted as a checkpoint, as a translator or informer, reviewing my scores and performance, achievements, and advancements with perfect accuracy. We are all an expression of the same source, the same consciousness, with as many expressions as one could imagine; we have the tools, we're given the opportunity, and then try to understand what they can be used for.

The power of imagination is a powerful tool to help us create, expand, and explore our capacities. Our Spirit has connections to the cosmos, with endless information, potential, and energy, ready to connect you if you only listen carefully. It's perfection, it's love, it's beauty, it's growth, it's evolution—and we all have it in us. We are Spirit, expressed through the vehicle of our body while on earth.

This Entity approached me. We hovered together on clouds with that bluish white light surrounding us, and it was a bit hazy. He came closer, and I could see he was definitely older than me and embodied enormous knowledge. He was very experienced in these circuits, full of energy and defined purpose, with no time to lose. Thus, he looked at me, and the most amazing thing happened.

He knew I was ready, eager, and hungry for what came next as we work like magnets. Out of substance in different density he pulled something like a folder with my information. It was clearly my file, as if it read in big, bold letters: Earth Life Experience File. He sent it to me in an invisible ball of energy. I accepted and received the light with all its content. The information came in a condensed form and progressively opened up as I started absorbing it into my consciousness. This was the beginning of what I can best define as telepathy, and from that moment onwards this is how we communicated.

This dense energy file opens up a transparent screen section between us. We could both see it, and a large sequence of images flashed across the screen. Both of us watched, frame by frame, and evaluated the main message of each episode in the movie of my life. Beginning at the moment I joined my body, I felt the emotions and growth of each manifestation, each episode. I relived each experience, feeling the memory as if it had just happened. Scenes went by at a fast pace, but at the same time, it was steady enough to take it all in. I had the sensation that the past, present, and future were all there at the same time, side by side. We saw it all, understanding each decision and its consequence, acknowledging, exchanging perceptions, and perspectives in between us, again, by telepathic understanding.

We were watching it, reading into it and imagining other possible outcomes. As if watching a motion picture, I thought about the *what ifs* of making different choices. Instead of subtitles, the information was instantaneously absorbed and understood. My story was narrated, detail after wonderful detail. It was captivating to see the events leading to each moment. All the information was presented as presently happening. As we lived the episode, we traveled in place and felt it happen. Thus, we better understood the reasons behind the decisions, understanding how both the memory and the event are present simultaneously, just in a different vibrational dimension. Everything was here now, with clarity. I was in a blissful state.

Gaining Clarity

Awareness. It's all about awareness. You make your choices based on the knowledge you have in you. The old expression, "If I knew then what I know now," comes to mind. These pictures were charged with profound meaning; a life compressed into one movie. It really makes you wonder: if each of our lives are stored in a file, in pictures compressed like a zip file that can be relived, are computers and programs just a physical extension of how this process really works?

Which other dimensions interlocked in the same fabric of this universe can we not hear or see? Abilities? Spaces? Layers? Zones? Dimensions? What might be hidden from sight and touch but not from Spirit if asked for? In this perspective we need an open mind for what's coming, hinting that we are ready to receive it. In the asking, it is given. The fact is, it doesn't matter what has been my past, what has been written or stated as a fact in the physical world, for now I had left that singular experience to bring the message with me: You owe nothing to anyone. You are much more. You are everything you want to be. You are here to have fun, to enjoy and be creative about it. You have a birthright to happiness, bliss, and fulfilment. You can be, do, and have anything you want. Follow your gut feeling and be happy. There is no death. Follow your joy. Trust the voice within. I gained all these from this experience, along with many other clarities of thought. I was loving the fact I'd been chosen for this. I was chosen to be called to this meeting with creative purposes and rights, and sent back down to earth to clarify as many as I could, if not just by example. Trust your powers.

Some episodes I remembered, and some I didn't, but all of them were explained as if I was watching someone else's story and not my own. I saw all the decisive moments through the years, all my crossroads and choices, all the clever moves—and the fuckups. In the end, there are no mistakes, only things we want to experience. It all made sense. This Supreme Being was cleaning up my life, by changing my perspective on it, offering me the insight of hindsight. I learned about where I came from, how I was born, my family environment, their origins and agendas, our paradigm, why I chose them, and future plans. I found clarification; a stronger sense of being and self-worth. A relief in being who I am regardless of the circumstances and opinion.

I gained clarity around moments I didn't otherwise remember, and that made a huge difference. I'd feel the memory, see the date, and the story as I experienced it at that time. What a phenomenal opportunity to make the most of it, focusing on the positive side of the event. I dealt with the challenges, understanding, forgiving, loving, accepting, and moving on with gratitude to the next moment. And so, on and on this experience went, filtering through the ups and downs of my current timeline.

I found answers to my questions: *Why did this happen? Why did I choose this? Who did that to me? Was this good for me? What did I do wrong? What did I do right? Who did that, and why?* All my questions were answered! And with every experience, I relived the emotion and connected to the pain, joy, or elation. We cleared memories, cleaned them up, similarly to *Ho'oponopono* (the Hawaiian practice of reconciliation and forgiveness): I'm sorry. Please forgive me. Thank you. I love you. It was as if we applied this concept to the necessary moments in order to clear my past and freely move forward. Visiting, filtering, enlightening the way. I had no guilt or shame, only understanding. Emotion comes from the mind, not from Spirit. Emotion is the result of our mental activity. Again, we feel bliss when in Spirit; it is perfect, all-knowing and understanding. It doesn't react, rather, it responds. Emotion doesn't encompass it though emotion is the main part of life on this earthly experience. It's why we come here, to live emotions and grow with them.

Occasionally, we paused my life review to focus on decisive events that needed additional clarification. I was able to give time to each moment for more careful interpretation. Most of these events which lasted a millisecond in my recollection, such as meeting a stranger or a lover on a street corner for a talk or lengthy dinner, were now turning points in my life. I was given the gift of reliving each and every experience, knowing very well the impact they had on my future.

As we develop a new idea and become excited, take action on it and persist, it will eventually bring us to the door of opportunity. As a ripple effect, the universe responds by opening the door for a change, proving once more that we create our own path. We build the doors we want to open, and then, with courage, faith, and good will, we can walk directly through them. The process never fails. We paused for these events, these turning points, so to speak; the moments that eventually determine if, years later, you'll be taking the taxi or the limo, the train or the chopper, by yourself or with a family of five.

These moments make up the narratives of our lives. Connecting to our instinct and listening to intuition are crucial practices in living a life of pure excitement. This is believing in and using our body and mental faculties as they are designed to be used—for our greater good. Our mind, our consciousness, and our bodies are all connected to the same thing. They all communicate with one another. The least we can do is give this perfect system the credit it deserves and actually listen to it. We have a major guest living with us (Spirit), visiting us; we want to give this special guest a five-star experience!

Nature is perfect. We are nature, and we are perfect. We have to trust our instinct, our heart, and our intuition. Doing so will prepare us for any eventuality. While we're working with nature, we know that everything will flow easily, at the right pace, as it's the only way.

As I watched the movie unfold, I realized the undeniable importance of decisions. Sometimes we find that the entire

our life is determined by one single decision. We
n stories, we're faced with options (let's be hon-
ving options), then comes the moment to make a
decision. Do we honor it because we know it's what we utterly
love? Do we bail? Can we be influenced by others? Of course,
we can. Are they the best influences? Not always. Sometimes
yes, sometimes no. Knowing what I know, only one choice is
the best for us as we listen to our inner being. Follow your joy!
Did we give the right amount of attention to all the decisions
we made? Did we decide intuitively on the spot? I love those
decisions of inspired action! Maybe yes! Our entire existence is
dependent on the decisions we make, as well as those we don't.
The practice of making decisions is constantly unfolding. Some
choices are easy, like what to eat for dinner. Others are more
difficult, like whether you should get married or start your own
business. The truth is, when we're aligned with our inner being
for our highest good, all choices are easy. We know intuitively
what's best for us.

Successful people make the decision to be successful long
before they actually start walking. They don't accept anything
other than success. I see success as a person who satisfies his
own desires. It's not even a question; it's a state of being, a desire,
or a core existential knowing. It's a must, a fact that accompa-
nies the thought: *there's no way I won't succeed.* Making the right
decisions at the right time becomes an instinctive habit. You'll
intuitively know how to handle situations that once baffled
you. Deciding what's best will become natural; you'll just know,
and you will do it. I love this transition in life, when we come
to the point of making decisions based on instinct and intuitive

knowledge. Some people are born with this ability while others need to train it over time.

As you follow and trust in your intuition, you're acting out of faith, feeling the idea, visualizing, getting emotionally involved with it and moving forward on to it. In that moment when you know which decision to make, take the risk and put it into action. You get excited, and this high vibration changes everything. It changes the scenario as you attract the right circumstances. Everything works out, and you succeed because you decided it would be so. You chose the end result, you transformed your vision into reality.

The universe loves this and responds to your beliefs, making you feel like the fantastic creator that you are. Since you received your desired result, you can build your self-confidence and expand your awareness. This snowball effect of positivity continues to grow as much as you want it to and for however long you let it. You'll continue manifesting your desires, and that's success. Our thoughts drive us into the person we want to become. Our decisions make us who we want to become, building character as they shape us into the higher level of self. And as you know, if its acting out of joy, everything else will flow on to you, satisfying beyond expectations.

Together with Entity, we watched my life's review. We continued on, watching and pausing, watching and pausing, over and over again. As the slide show of my life is shared with this ethereal presence, my mind was free from doubt. I was humbled and filled with respect for life and for the operators behind the curtain. We're all energy—moldable, adaptable energy.

Awash in Gratitude

I felt inundated with gratitude like never before. Plenitude, and profound gratitude. I felt gratitude for the gift I had just received, gratitude for the experience, gratitude for the connection, gratitude for just *being*. I was grateful for the insight into all the choices that made me who I am. Grateful for realizing what kind of person I could become now, starting clean, and having seen how to use the laws to make it work well. I learned that not only could I connect to the Supreme Intelligence, the Source of all life, but I could also look inside for guidance, as my soul is also an extension of the Supreme Source. We all are. I learned that I can make a new choice about who I want to be and how I want to live. I knew how to connect, from where to obtain the information, and who to listen to and follow for guidance on a purely joyful life. It was all there. It had always been. I just didn't see it before. Now, it's here.

I secured a new sense of clarity with each passing episode. The reassurance and peace of mind that came with this experience was enlightening to say the least. It made me stronger, cleaner, and more powerful. By *powerful*, I mean spiritually independent and self-reliable. As the review continued, I absorbed all of the precious information, downloading, acknowledging, remembering, forgiving, loving, and resetting my mind and soul with more and more gratitude. Suddenly, I visualized my body as I left it. For a fraction of a second I was sad and worried about dying; then, not anymore. I felt the plenitude of my new position and released all concern. I felt how I could help from here, from the non-physical world. I was blissful in this spiritual form, and there was no need to look back. Funny how the recognition of my body flat in front of the garage didn't matter anymore, like it was something from a very different past. I cherished it, I acknowledged it, I knew him very well, we've been through a lot together—but he was old news now. Now I was focused on being in the new dimension.

The sequence ended with us looking at the narrative that led to my heart attack, revisiting my soul's journey through life right up until that moment. The Entity clearly explained what caused the death of my body in the same clear manner that he explained everything that had happened before. He told me how it was activated, what triggered it, what forces were at play, and how my mind and body reacted to it all. How I have allowed it to come to me; how I created and attracted it into my experience. Hard truths were exposed. He showed me my place according to the perspective of my family, what they saw in me, what they projected, and what they expected of me. I saw the chain reaction between the emotional conflicts resulting in that sudden end. Yes, there had been hate. Yes, there was revenge. And yes, there was difference of opinion. All could have been avoided. Yes, it could have. I could have ignored it and moved on, but I didn't. Perspective influenced my emotions. The idea and feelings of rejection were too big and too disappointing, which led to my thoughts, and therefore, the physical consequences in my body. I had manifested it, wished for it, called for death and death came running. I'd learnt firsthand the true power of desire, focus, and the emotions associated with thought. A mental suicide, and the body reacted to it.

If we knew the power of our thoughts, we wouldn't dare think a negative thought again. Thoughts are very powerful and are boosted by our emotions. Think well and love, and you'll have a beautiful life!

Everyone has a similar chain reaction in the events and emotions of their life. We're all energy. We are all connected. Everything is connected in a whirlpool of electromagnetic existence and emotions all working together. As such, sometimes we rush, sometimes we love, and sometimes we react. That's all part of life. I learned it was my turn now to take it easy and savor the good things in life; the good rhythms, the good feelings, and the desired results. My soul had to visit the Creator's arms for a wake-up call, an update on my service on earth. I was lucky enough to receive a review from the top, a detailed analysis from the fantastic perspective of this Spiritual Entity working through Universal Consciousness, speaking with its purity, perfection, and authority. You can feel the power of creation as Spirit and soul make peace and recognize their place in the universe—or at least on this round rock in the Milky Way.

Words are not enough to explain the sensation of understanding, the feeling in acquiring this non-physical view of life and of our existence. The vibration is of the highest level and fantastic quality. The blissful sensation of rightful universal being. It is the state we should be in at all times. We have it in us. We are it. We just need to allow it. It's ours, mine, and yours. It's a flow of energy, a light passing through us, the center of the earth and the cosmos. Your Zenith will be exposed as you fearlessly take ownership, take charge, and dare through your passage in an enlightened way.

While out of body, I reached a new level of understanding: I Am; I am a soul; I am a spiritual being; I'm whole and connected. I'm so powerful I can create the reality I want to experience, I can move and change with one intention. I have abundance in my nature of everything that I desire. I'm graciously giving and gratefully receiving at once. I feel, now, and believe I'm ready to move into the next stage of my existence. I was okay now with all that happened, I understood how I came to that point of having a heart attack. I made peace and closed the earth project. I was *now*, abundantly being, flowing replenished, becoming acquainted with my surroundings and other souls I could see and feel not far away.

The soul doesn't die. Spirit is Eternal. The you that is you carries on beyond the veil until its next walk around the block when Spirit decides to join a newborn baby, or any other dimension we choose to service and grow. I know there are options after this stage. I saw other souls and Spirits flying around with purpose and direction. Were they waiting for a new role? For a new family? New challenges? Or were they already busy with the new assignments, preparing to enter yet another dimension? I don't know. They were there, and it wasn't for me to deal with, or at least not at this moment, as I was fully focused on that present moment concerning only myself.

We cover a lot of ground in a lifetime on earth. It is filled with emotions, relationships, experiences, and evolutions. After the review, I felt I could have done better. I thought: *Well ... I'm not done. I'd still like to do this and that, stay on earth longer, evolve more, expand and create. I'd like to come back and succeed, live better, share my voice, dare, risk, be my highest self, and leave my signature.* I didn't want to die just yet. I wanted to enjoy life on earth with more excitement, higher vibrations, and better experiences. I understood now that being here alive is a fantastic gift, an opportunity to experiment and develop the great scheme of things; We have a role in the in Universe, not just at work. I valued it more now seeing the connections. I got a new respect for the opportunity of smelling the earth and watching a sunrise, feeling the wind or holding hands in love and agreement! Looking back made me see how good Life really is.

As we reached the end of the presentation, I felt peaceful, powerful, and confident to a point where I had no more questions. Immediately after, the Entity said, "Yes, this is all you, and yes, you've been through a great deal of emotional conflict and it's not your time to come here yet. You will now experience joy, love, plenitude and bliss! You have a lot to go through. You have a bright and beautiful side of life that is yours to fully live, embrace, feel the potential of, and live it to the fullest of your true abilities as co-creator and habitant of this system. You will continue. You're going to your body again and this time you're in blissful presence. You're in joy, you're in happiness, you're going to follow your excitement, you're going to succeed and be great, and you're never looking back."

He carried on explaining what he wanted me to do once back in my physical body. Immediately, a "to-do list" popped in my consciousness that I would resolve utilizing the powerful tools of being a spirit, utilizing the soul's abilities to live well. I had just learned the mechanics of the system I'd been distracted from, reinforcing the idea that I didn't owe anything to anyone. I could focus on myself. The world was mine to evolve and I wouldn't be alone, he would be there for me; I could create the life I desired, preferably by not hurting anyone in the process.

He graciously shared endless information, explaining where I should not go both mentally and physically, what not to think about, what to care for, what matters, how to carry on, and what to ignore. He communicated with such precision that I didn't doubt him for a fraction of a second. I uncovered the powers of our existence, the powers of thought. Human energy and emotion are much stronger than what most believe. I was profoundly grateful. The imagery of my life's review had ended, and I stared at the all-knowing Entity. We connected and exchanged telepathic charges, acknowledging blocks of information with a fantastic vibe. We both clearly felt each other's intentions. We are happy, satisfied in the energy of one another. The respect and acknowledgement of pure love. We were done. We had finished our exchange, at least for the time being.

I was complete and didn't really want to let go of that feeling. Imagine gaining such knowledge from the Source of Life, getting in touch with it, feeling the fountain of life vibrations, and realizing *that's* who you are —a vibrant, life energy fountain, an overflow of pure, white light energy, healthy and perfect. From this feeling, plants grow, birds fly, trees breed, water flows, and life moves on evolving and expanding. The energy is so perfect. Our planet spins at the perfect speed, the perfect distance, and in the perfect rhythm around the sun. All this happens in a galaxy inside a universe and all of it just is, as you are, growing and totally pure.

We can use our intelligence—rather, our imagination, our thoughts, and our feelings—to create our future life. We create it, even if we don't know of it, even if we don't agree or believe in it. It cannot be stopped. We are creating our lives all the time:

now, and now, and now! On this planet, you experience any-thing you believe in; manifestation is a default ability we have, that's why we're here for. Your beliefs and your expectations will create your reality, your experience. That's how powerful you and your thoughts are. So, take the time! Change beliefs in order to manifest something good for yourself, and conse-quently for those you love! Joy is the goal!

This is super-hero style. Imagine we can manipulate this energy around us with our thoughts and boost it with our focused feelings into creation, into e-motion. In a direct rela-tionship with the ether, we manipulate the molecules that bring our thoughts into reality through an electromagnetic mixture of invisible substances. Call it magic, call it science, call it metaphysics. It doesn't matter what you call it because you're using it, now.

Do you see how powerful this is, how grateful we should be? We're given the chance to feel our lives into existence. We can create the lives we want. We can imagine it, think it, feel it, and bring it into existence out of thin air to our experience and satisfaction. And that's living. That's using the powers given to us. I'm forever grateful for this experience, for the opportu-nity to have taken this class on life's fabrics one on one. I love this, and I know why I received it. Since I was a young child, I was intrigued by it. I was curious and wanted to know how life works, and so I got the answers. Ask, believe, receive. I got it because I always wanted to use it, and I always wanted to share with others the wonders of our existence, even if at the time I only had questions. I got it because it's where and who I am. It's my essence, and it's okay!

Spirit is *perfect*. It's in you. For a few moments, I was at the purest version of myself, until yesterday, as more is coming. The best version of anything, for that matter. We are each equipped with this magnificent setting of body, brain, mind, soul, consciousness, and imagination, with an electrical current running free through each of us. We're connected. What are we going to do? What can we do? What do you want to do? We are powerful creative beings in a human body.

Unfortunately, through the ages, the amazing, creative, positive souls on earth have endured dark and negative outcomes—perhaps proof of the Law of Polarity: *Everything has an opposite. Up and down, hot and cold, in and out, and so on.* Polar opposites make existence possible, and that's one of the characteristics of this planet—*duality.* If what you are not did not coexist with what you are, then what you are could not be. It's the second time in this book I mention this law, and I find it one of the least explored. But yet, it is a very satisfying one. I wonder, can good exist without evil? I learned the definition of evil as "that which is not in alignment with the things we want." Can peace exist without war? Yes, I believe we can experience one without the other. We can do it. Focus on the good, focus on the laughter, focus on the abundance of flourishing forests, happy children, plenty of food, and plenty of money. Focus on the positive and you will create it. A clean abundant planet, fruit, fish, birds, eco-friendly villages, cities, civilization, and technology with a heart. It is so simple. We must begin to ignore what was created negatively and start believing and visualizing how good it can be, how good it can become, with all this potential. Paradise was given to us; we abused it somewhat, and the timing is perfect for us to make it the best generational experience ever. Scientific knowledge and spiritual discoveries working together. I'm so happy and excited with what's to come.

Matching Vibrations

It's clear why and how wars begin, how they manifest in the physical and how far we have brought them with so much technology; we are killing our own species! Sudden ego-based reactions of the mind start a vicious cycle of survival or greedy narratives. It is thought with emotion thereby attracting its vibrational equivalent. Okay, things got a bit out of hand. I have no doubt that in the greater scheme of things it was a necessary area of growth and experience. With conflict, great solutions take place. Not because we want them to, but because the vibrations must match. It's flawless. It works whether we want it to or not; it responds with its vibrational match of prolonged thought and emotion. It matches out of consequence, cause, and effect. It's the proof that the system works, we can use it intelligently for a dream life. There is no connotation in good or bad in the Spirit dimension. Only a man's interpretation makes it good or bad, meaning, the good or bad depends entirely on us. We're given the tools, but why are we doing this? Do children need to suffer? Do adults need to suffer? Do we need to destroy the planet's resources? This was the main reason I wanted to drop LSD in every person's meal, water bottle, or even in the city's main supply. I wanted to inundate the so-called *civilized* corporate world with the peace and love portal to a life of praise. Obviously, didn't do it. The concept of winning and losing, when taken personally,

will eventually fade away giving room to the nat'
edgement that we are enough. We are more th
live naturally.

The good thing is, we can focus on the opposite; we can focus
on what we want in order to create a better world. Peace, love,
harmony, abundance, appreciation, and flourishing nature.
Positive thinking is not a cliché—it's a *must*. Think positively
and you'll see immediate results in your day-to-day life. We can
foresee the world as we want it. Yes, advanced technologically
within the Cosmic Laws. Ancient scriptures reveal the use of
Light and Sound Technology; electromagnetism to move matter, stones, using the sun for laser techniques. We have been
more advanced. Accept it.

If the Law of Polarity states that two sides are present in the
same object, can we avoid it? Must we have pain to recognize
joy? Can we live in peace, abundance, and development without
the dark side of war? Can we focus and live only on the positive
side of this law? Are these polarities growing in proportion? Is
it even physically possible? Yes, I think it is, and I think we can;
it reminds me of another Universal Law which has been one of
my best friends. I made it a priority since facing an extended
and almost complete change in myself. Change involves resistance. The Law of Non-Resistance states: *Every thought has a
frequency. The less you resist something, the less it will exist. By not
focusing on the resistance you will have the success that you want.*
Basically, if and when we resist a condition, a person, or a thing
we don't like or want, we are in fact giving power to that thing.
Thoughts are energy, and resisting will only make them bigger, as if you're feeding the beast that you're fighting against.

All we have do is to think of what we want. Easy. Only feed the life you want to live. Let the beast starve and it will disappear. Personally, it didn't matter if it sounded like cowardly or selfish behavior, for it was the most intelligent thing to do in dealing with unpleasant situations. I focus on the outcome that I desire.

On the other hand, if the concepts of good and bad only depend on perspective, as things merely do (recall the Law of Relativity: *Nothing is good or bad until we relate it to something),* then we, as the creators of each, take full responsibility. John Lennon wrote one of my favorite songs, "Instant Karma," where he speaks cleverly and beautifully on this subject. It's solely on us. It's up to you and me to determine what we get out of life. The coin has two sides, which one do you want to see every day? You can choose! Everything we experience is a consequence of our thoughts, individually and collectively agreed on. When the collective mind focuses on the beautiful, bright constructive world, like a domino effect, we have almost instant manifestations matching those vibrations. Usually, the easier action takes prevalence over the more difficult tasks, and I blame it on alcohol. If you don't drink, it's easier to keep a positive and high loving vibration. You intuitively appreciate life, creating more of it. As Abraham Hicks says, "When you focus on the good, the good gets better." We're definitely a work-in-progress species!

With today's knowledge, it has never been more important to find balance in the connection between thought and feeling. There is no excuse because we know what we have to do, and we know how to do it. Our ability to create a fantastic life without disturbing our neighbors is proven by the law of cause and effect. It's a choice, and we know it. Spirit is everywhere, love is abundant, and peace is within reach. The Law of Attraction delivers it, whether we're aware of it or not. Status quo is manmade; it's a mind creation and not spiritual. Spirit is love, unlimited, understanding. When accepted and developed in the right way, we thrive effortlessly. Maybe it's the Law of Gestation working at a grander scale. Or maybe it's in the gestations stage, and it's taking its time to manifest this idea of a flourishing and thriving world where technology, spirituality, and nature flow together with ease and joy. The Law of Gestation states: *Everything takes time to manifest. All things have a beginning and grow into form as more energy is added to them. Focus on ideals and they will become reality when the time is right.* There is a natural order of things, and knowing this is one more reason to relax and enjoy the ride; do the mind work, daydream, visualize, feel it, think it, and let it come to be. It will be delivered.

The elevation of consciousness, its awareness, and the knowledge on this matter goes far beyond my conception of it; but I do ponder it. We can only guess and wonder where we really are for now. It's funny how we find answers when we continue to search for them. I know I would have never gone through this spiritual experience if I hadn't been so curious about it from a young age. *Where do we come from? What for? How much, and what can we achieve?* One of Napoleon Hill's most famous quotes comes to mind: "What the mind can conceive and believe, it can achieve." Or, as Bob Proctor regularly states, "If you can see it in your mind, you can hold it in your hand." Yes, one hundred percent, search and you will find. As many other teachers from many different backgrounds eventually dropped some short but sweet truths, the only way to explain it is through personal experience. My point being: whatever you're curious about, go for it. Don't ignore your inner call, your signature, as this might have been the main reason you came to the planet this time anyway!

Live a life of excitement, plenitude, expansion, development, and gratitude. I want to be in direct connection to the light, to be a channel of love, the source of our life, because I choose to. It excites me to know what I am made of and that I can change my experience. Well, I can change the frequency of that which I'm made of, and that change of frequency will dictate how I live my life. This is directly connected to the Law of Vibration: *Everything vibrates, and nothing rests. Vibrations of the same frequency resonate with each other. Like energy attracts like energy. Everything is energy, including our thoughts.* Choose a frequency, or, choose an ideal and match that frequency. Ask for it and then let it come. Watch the magic happen! I found that pure loving vibration in all that is, the Life Source. I carried it everywhere most of the time, imbedded in my veins, and nothing could take that experience away from me. I humbly and gratefully kept myself in that righteous feeling of bliss that we're entitled to, and my life began to change, attracting more and more reasons to be happy about! There was one other thing was missing in this process, as I found regularly until some point in my life. The area that needed more work at the subconscious level— the *allowing*.

I had to learn "allowing" it to be and "allowing" the receiving of my best present life. Allowing my best *now*. This came with self-love and a good self-image; the self-worth values I had were dictating how much was I allowing myself to receive. Since the encounter with my Entity, my self-worth changed completely. I love myself now so much, I could give myself anything I wanted, I deserve it, and I allow myself to receive it now, and allowing myself to be the person I saw in me, and enjoy it. Now that I knew what to do, I'd allow myself to receive all the good things I desired and asked for! It's about me taking care of me. It's an amazing life with a perfect system. Keep yourself in the vibration of what you want to receive, and you will receive it!

This doesn't mean I didn't give to others if they ask. I'd still wished that everyone had what they desired, as we'd raise the overall planet's mood and vibration. That would be the goal, to bring the planet to a lighter, happier, easier, and gratifying evolution.

I mention the Universal Laws regularly, and you can find them everywhere online and in bookstores. Dr. Raymond Holliwell has a fantastic book on a selected few of them. I was lucky enough to do a coaching program where we studied these laws for months. I continue to study them so they may be permanently implant them in my DNA—to live them as naturally as I breathe.

The fact remains that we lead the way. The mind allows the entry of Spirit into our thinking, into our conscious decision-making progress, allowing us to co-create the reality we want for ourselves. Trusting and allowing ourselves to make it well; guiding and growing humanity in a conscious direction. It's trust that we need now. Everything gets a billion times better if and when we allow Spirit to guide us. All the power in the universe can be used for good. It's limitless, pure, and it's yours. We can be the best generation this planet has ever known.

Returning now to my time with the Entity—we finished watching my journey through earth in a blissful state. With each passing moment, I learned a tremendous amount of information about myself, my life, my journey, and my direction. I always felt and thought I'd be involved in magic, aliens, fantasy, or non-physical areas of my experience. But never did I think I would meet such an Entity. But there I was, analyzing the book of my life and receiving remarkable insight. On some level I must have expected it, otherwise it wouldn't have happened. It was a phenomenal experience, although something tells me that it may be a recurrent event, or at least that I should keep the communication channel open. Meeting with the Supreme beings offered me something that no physical experience could parallel. To this day, I still feel blessed and privileged for the opportunity to meet and connect with such a mentor. I am humbled by the knowledge and experience of a fifth-dimensional episode. I'm forever grateful for the review, the reset, and the enlightenment it produced within me. Thank you.

The concept of "life after death" had been one of my favorite topics from a young age. I often stared at the night sky feeling "I've been here before ..." I always had a happy and relaxed approach to it; there was a "it will be fine" feeling, but it was a hunch, a suspicion. Now, I know it, I believe. It's a fact. We exist, we change place, we create. Now I felt that I was in a blank slate, ready to be crafted into a magnificent work of art to my choosing. What would come next? Would I descend back to land and reacclimate with my old body? Or would I take new form, something unfamiliar yet exciting—a fresh start? Who knew?

Regardless, I could only pray that my conscious awareness would follow, filled with fresh insight. This *knowing* couldn't be wasted, for now I knew things I could only dream of and had acquired information few others could ever acquire. I had a new sense of self, armed with the insight of a million decisions. My first kiss, first bike ride, first love, first drink, first drug use, first victory, first prize received, first everything—all dealt with and taken care of, not to worry about it ever again. It was now clear how easily all of this unfolds, and with it I was ready to start creating, choosing, and enjoying. Thick or thin, loaded with love, light, and pure Spirit, I would make all my dreams a reality.

Chapter 5

The Ticket

Conscious awareness of love energy and accepting
that I am loved. I deserve!

eeling blissfully pure, forgiven, open in a clear sense of
mind and spirit, I was well-connected in a rooted and
unlimited way. I could feel myself again, my soul was
complete. In a pure state, vibrating as a body of energy, clean,
without any added "pollution" in my thoughts or emotion. I
could clearly see and feel all areas: soul, mind, and consciousness. We're now at the stage where I realize I'm going back to
physical form; I'm not staying in this beautiful and amazing
dimension. But yet we're still here, facing each other. We were
not done after all, there's more!

I could feel a load of information coming, because I was asking
for it. I was now ready to receive it, I had space for it, I was in the

vibrational alignment of receiving. He continued, in a similar tone or plane of action as before. There was a sense of mission now. It wasn't that he was allowing me, but more like he was giving me an order: *You have to go back, and this is what you have to do: You're going to have the time of your life. You will create it with fun and love. You're going to expand incredibly, following Joy. You're going to imagine a new world and live it. You're going to grow with excitement. You're going to have the abundance that is yours and fulfillment in achieving the desired life that is for you. You are a source of joy, love, and light, so act like it.* It was guidance, but with strict clarity. It wasn't an order, but it felt like an one, and I didn't want to disappoint, disobey, or ignore him. I had received guidance from above—I got the message.

He gave me a different perspective of my entire presence on earth; a big shift in how I perceived everything. The reason we were still here is because we were missing important details that make all the difference. He told me how to deal with and how to behave toward specific people, including family, friends and acquaintances. He then very clearly stated, *You're going now. You have to go. It's time to move on.* And in a flash of movement and energy I was off, flying back to land. Ffffeeeeeewwwww

Through the Entity's perspective, it was as if my entire presence on earth was now "sponsored." There was a new view in all areas, including my journey through the psychedelic valleys of consciousness and creation, which I didn't consider a mistake anymore (and they proved valuable for my current experience). It was all related to my soul's essence, my core beliefs of unconditional love, peace, compassion, embracing nature, and providing for all.

The lesson in detachment left a huge impression on me. How easy and how important it is to detach. You don't need to hold on to the things that don't bring you happiness. Instead, detach. Detach from narratives that don't serve you, detach from material things that don't add joy, detach from people who don't love the way you want to be loved, detach from the old ways, detach from memories, detach from the past, detach from socially accepted and politically correct behaviors, detach from the norm and all institutionalized rules, as none of it makes you feel better. To make room for the New Earth we need to let go of the old.

Accept events, learn from them, and take the good. Forgive and let go. Remember, what you own ends up owning you. So, give them away! Plus, the more you give the more space you create and the universe gives back. Let go and appreciate. Appreciate how beautiful life is. Appreciate the trees, your pets, animals, the oxygen, and the clouds. Appreciate how beautiful it is to be alive, to make love, or to meet someone you click with. Praise and love the things that makes you happy. Praise your health, and praise anything that brings you joy!

I had to let go of the old me so that I could create space for the new me. Being in contact with the Supreme Intelligence created a clear impression that I had to break away from my social habitat. My old self literally died. This is a whole new me. It's clearly the Law of Sacrifice at work here: *To give up something of a lower nature for something of a higher nature.* As it is a Universal Law, it's always at work whether we believe in it or not, like all the other Laws mentioned in this book. This clearly means that we must let go of something old if we want something new. One of my mentors, Bob Proctor (if you have studied self-development, you'll be familiar with Bob Proctor. He has been doing this for 59 years now), states regarding this Law: "In order to enjoy extraordinary success in life, we have to sacrifice our time, put in the effort and be disciplined to work for the things we want to achieve. We have to be persistent and persevere to work for what we want in order to achieve it." I had to let go of a everything I was doing before! We need to change habits. We need to identify and remove the leg cuffs that restrain our forward movement. In my case, I was sacrificing what had once identified me as the person I was in order to become who I can and want to be.

If you're born in a typical social environment or large family group, you get a label and a set of characteristics. You're a piece of that puzzle. You're there. It's decided: *this is who you are; this is how you behave.* It will be like that forever unless you choose to decide differently. Humans like to label things in order to better understand what they are, as it gives us security to define them. You become labeled, and you're expected to develop into the role that fits that label. You might think, "That's not who I am!" But even so, you continue to play that role until the day you've had enough of pleasing others and decide to move on in order to please your soul and catch up on lost time. Don't wait for the lid to blow up! Do it Now!

The danger is to accept the ascribed identity. I did this for many years without even imagining a different possibility. I accepted the circumstances and labels. I numbed my brain from curative thought and followed directions. I lived life in the shadow of the expectations and principles of others. I'm not complaining or being ungrateful—I loved my upbringing, and I'm forever grateful for those years. I was blessed. But there is a point where we have to think for ourselves. Life is too short to be living someone else's dreams.

The risk of giving advice is that we are influencing the younger generations. We give the best advice we know and have pure intentions, but we never know the impact. Maybe some people should stay where they are born and fill that role without questioning, and that's great too. Who am I to question their role? But I needed to go!

In my situation, the path of adolescence took me through a sequence of anti-establishment ideas. I was very revolutionary, I was a punk, and I went from failure to failure without questioning. I was a destroyer, mainly of myself but also of opportunity. I was angry. It took a lot of pain to discover, accept, believe, and receive the concept that life is a fantastic gift. I had to lose my life in order to realize how much I actually loved it. It took a heart attack to see how lovable I am! It showed me how good I am, how much I love myself, and how much I love life. I had to be reborn into a new mission and turn my life around. I had to let go of my whole previous self so that I could create the one I'm meant to be.

Going forward, I resolved to focus on myself as a perfect being who deserves a fantastic time on earth. As above, so below.

While the behavior of my teenage years helped me grow in some areas—using drugs in large quantities while seeking love, answers, and companionship—they also hindered my growth and expansion in society's terms. My behavior created obstacles and stifled possibilities. But perhaps those behaviors played the part they were meant to play in order to bring me here today, to write this book, and share with others so that they can also find their full self-worth without going through a path of self-destruction. They say smart people learn through their own mistakes while intelligent people learn from the mistakes of others. Be that as it may, I now have my ticket to a Fantastic World. It's been well-paid for, earned, and given to me with the knowledge that the more people I can help, the better employed this ticket will be.

The Upside of Failing

The good side to failure is that you become closer to getting it right. Actually, I'd like to replace "failure" with "learning." There is no failure, only growth. You learn and you get to know yourself better. You become empowered and self-confident. If I needed to go through all of that to be the person I am today, I'd do it. I loved it. I like to think that the Entity worked as my Spirit Guide, my Mentor. It makes sense and intuition tells me so. I should have asked his name.

Let me make one thing clear: This is not a complaint, I loved my childhood and I loved what my parents provided for me. However, I realized that some parents do a better job of driving their children in the right direction to become great, to change the world, to follow their dreams, and be all they can be. And that's fantastic, so hats off to them. Honestly desiring and supporting your kids to be the best versions of themselves takes a great heart. I presume those parents are in tune with Spirit and connected to the Supreme Intelligence. When a mix of love and imagination acts within you and through you that has inspired action, phenomenal results can occur. There are other types of kids, too—those who have a calling that they can't stop chasing. They go for it and win big even through the ups and downs! Then there are those kids who take time to wonder and evaluate where they are. They feel a bit lost and pulled sideways, and it takes a fight to gain control over their lives. Maybe that's the Law of Sacrifice at play again. You do have to train a lot to win a medal in the Olympics!

I truly love my family. They gave my brothers and myself care, love, affection, wonderful experiences, and companionship. They also taught me how to drink and party, and maybe I liked it too much or took it a bit too far. I don't blame them. They were sons of a different age! I now know the truth that I chose them to be my parents. I chose to be born then and there, and I chose the circumstances. This is not blaming, rather, fact checking as a growth process, they were doing their job greatly and that's why I chose them to be my parents.

As a kid, I was a bit different from others who held more concrete, steady plans. I was a daydreamer, a wonderer with an inquisitive mind for the abstract and all things metaphysics. Everything was possible as a child. I'd daydream about all my imaginable achievements. Now, I'm aware that we can tremendously improve our life as co-creators and that ambition is not a crime. No one should feel offended if a younger soul wants more from life. My parents gave me a fantastic life, I just wanted more. I wanted something different, and something that was exciting. I now understand that wanting more is a natural desire life. Life wants more. Life wants better. The universe itself wants more—it's constantly expanding. The jungle wants to grow more. The desire for more is a natural gift. I know that I chose my parents as the entry door to life on the tri-dimensional physical world, but I didn't know that at seventeen. That's why I'm grateful for the part my parents played. Bless them!

Near-death experiences can be very powerful. They have a way of jarring you awake. The Creator's messenger told me to free my mind, explore, develop without restrictions, and expand myself by following intuition. This was music to my ears! It gave me *carte blanche* to do whatever I wanted. It was as if I had been arrested by mistake for a crime I didn't commit, and was now being given everything I wanted in compensation. This feeling flooded me with the courage and enthusiasm needed to do everything I ever dreamed of, backed up by Universal Intelligence. This was empowering.

I had so much I wanted to do already. I was excited. I had a mission, and no one could put me down or take it away from me. The first thing I had to do was recover from this massive heart attack. I was left with a scar and 31 percent of the muscle was not working, so there were adjustments to be made. I had to disconnect, heal, and relax. I had to recover physically, mentally, and spiritually while scaling my priorities. Then, and only then, with a strong mind, strong body, and a courageous soul, could I take action and not look back.

Use Powerful Self Talk

A great sense of satisfaction came over me as I thought, *I knew it! I knew I could dream big. I knew I could be big. I knew it. My dreams were legit and not just fantasy. That was all real!* Freedom sets in. Gratitude took over. An order from the Source to explore without limitation awakes your imagination. It empowers you, as something you've intuitively suspected from a young age has been proven to be true. You know it and believe in it to the point where the unlimited universe shows you the starry nights and your innermost thoughts become a reality, independent of the opinions of others. I love it. Gratitude, freedom, and love for life all at once! Magical powers!

My self-talk changed instantly; I was now my best supporter, my biggest fan, and I had all of the positive inputs from the Source to fabricate the new personality I was developing. Most of the day was spent in a meditative state of empowering, visualizing, deciding, and being my best self. I knew I was on the right path picking up on my childhood pointers of my Soul's essence, my best decision and results, as they were straight from the Source. What was real to me, what belonged to my signature and original task, was now picked up and reinforced.

You find the reason for all the imagination and creativity in your younger self's inquisitive mind. That feeling and knowledge that you were part of something bigger, part of the big universe. We feel part of its expansion, just another ramification of its creative energy. Feeling the potential and the power of imagination supports our spirituality and our ambition to innovate. We grow, move forward, expand, express, and create without fear, only with excitement.

We share a vision and purpose that leads to humanity's great change, feeling the vibration that leads the way. We know we're doing the right thing because we can feel it. We have to take those moments and ideas, develop them, put them on paper, and practice them in order to manifest a plan and put it into motion. After all, we make our own reality. So why not make an incredible and a fantastic one? Why not make our lives a story worth telling? Why limit ourselves to what has already been done?

Imagination is the beginning of creation. For example, consider the first guy who made a chair out of wood. He was probably tired of sitting on a stone that hurt his backside. I can imagine the old, big tree that fell around his cave and how its wood eventually softened. On a break from hunting, this creator may have sat to enjoy a drink of water or to eat a rabbit. He visualized it. He thought of how he could carve a little seat. Then he thought to make it more comfortable, adding an arm rest or some cushions made from the skin of the fox he had eaten the week before. Those thoughts eventually turned to, *Hmmm ... how can I bring this sitting-tree to my wife so she can breastfeed my young son in comfort?* The ideas rushed in, and he eventually thought, *I know ... I'll cut the tree into smaller pieces and mount it back together in the cave.* He visualized it in his mind before he began cutting it into pieces. The power of imagination creates wonders!

My instructions were clear, concise, and powerful: follow joy, happiness, bliss, follow your dreams, and you can make them come true. Once you are in touch with this sort of personality, you are forever your own master.

It was time to follow my own way, in light with the universal conscious drive.

As you become fresh and clean from the source of knowledge, it's easy to follow its directions because you feel it's the only healthy way to live. It resonates with intuition and inner peace. It matches the unspoken truths and the natural rhythm all around you. This synchronicity develops courage and knowledge and reinforces the voice within that allows you to evolve, opening doors where before were only walls. For Spirit to express itself it requires quietness of the mind and action from the body to sow the necessary seeds and love. The intention to see the desired results and to feel them as a fact will bring them to experience. We are that powerful.

The Rewards of an Inspired Life

It takes awareness and courage to detach from the norm, ignore the naysayers, and carry on working on your desires and your chosen way of life. It matters what you do. Live your life, expand, create, and discover where you want to go in this experience we call life. If you do this, your intellect and character will follow.

The rewards of an inspired life are not only gratified by your own growth, but also multiplies the excitement as you inspire others. Risk to create your place among the most evolved species on earth. It is our duty to make the most of being here. We are given a fantastic gift at birth, and it's an offense to reject it or not use it to its fullest potential.

Living a life that is less than what we were created for leads to disease, wars, competition, and separation. If, instead, you live connected to your full potential, you can develop, evolve, ascend, assist, and create in line with mankind's duty, maximizing the gift and blessing of having so much opportunity.

Time is now my biggest commodity. There's none to lose. I feel and listen to this energy telling me to get up and get going. Go first, learn after, move, start walking—you'll intuitively know what to do by your creation, your intention, and ideas. In the backdrop, there was a vision for a peaceful society where people can coexist, live their dreams, create, and develop without war or misery. It is possible. It's doable. I've seen it. It's coming and it's not that far away; growing forests, a clean planet with incredible variety of animal life all flourishing again, oceans full of fish in a cleaner and healthier environment due to our high-tech knowledge and non-visible abilities.

At this point it seemed that the Spirit was asking, or at least I saw it as a request or a suggestion, for change of human expression. I felt he was looking for help to solve and avoid problems. He was looking for assistance in creating a peaceful world, with self-sufficient countries, happiness, and entertainment. Together we saw a beautiful world where the progress of science and technology aid Mother Nature and her living beings. Joy, nature, using the laws of physics with our minds, feeling the unseen. It was a fantastic revelation of bliss and unity, and again, I felt the important role that myself and all of us have in it.

As more topics came about, he continued to remind me to experience excitement and advancement. He emphasized the importance of the ecstasy of being, of joy, allowing happiness. That's the way to live! That's how humans must live life, in ecstasy, joy, and bliss. Go, do, and show. Not by explaining, but by being. Use the light, be the change, be joy. Regardless of the circumstances, be the example of possibility. I felt I had been given a massive message.

As the Spirit emphasized this message, I took it in and engraved it on my existence, never to forget. He then carried on to other details for safety and quick operation, like shortcuts and routes, ending with, *We're here. Listen to your intuition; do it, go for it, and don't look back.*

As he recited those powerful words, I felt recharged and refilled with the same energy that runs through and around us creating this flow of life. This is the energy of pure life, which is ever excelling. Once again, the concept of our origin becomes very clear. I can feel it, see it, and understand it. I see it radiating, a continuous swirling of the life energy that everything is made of.

I am grateful for the privilege of this event, this connection. As it ended, he seemed to be moving further away. However, I soon realized that he was stationary, and I was the one moving, moving back to earth. Falling backwards, I came down from the clouds with the same speed I had ascended. I was filled with the best feeling I've ever experienced, such bliss that I cannot compare it to any other. I felt purity and a righteous easiness all over me. I was full of light. I *was* light. I didn't have a care in the world, as everything had become clear. I excitedly wondered, *What's next?*

Chapter 6

Back on Land

The fine line between Spirit and the physical world,
here together. Now.

A s I descended, all of the new information was settling in.
I felt solid, together, and I knew where everything was as
if I had just tidied up a disorganized space. I could still
see my body on the ground in the same spot where I left it. I
would eventually find out, according to the doctors, my heart
attack was serious, causing over 31 percent of irreversible damage to my heart. The first cardiac arrest lasted between twenty
to twenty-five minutes. How did I survive? I was meant to.

I merge with my body. My two parts, flesh and soul, became one
again in the true Spirit of creation. When that merger occurred,
I had yet another incredible experience. I once again gained
form and became aware of my heavy physical body.

A Second Chance

I could clearly see that we have two separate thinking minds: the spiritual mind and the physical mind (brain). The brain can, in itself, divide between intuitive and rational, the latter with conscious and subconscious acts. They're different in the way they operate and think. One has no concerns or worries and knows everything is well and makes sense, while the other searches for riddles and justifications. As my brain came back online, all my other senses returned, and I could hear and taste again. I had lost these senses during my out-of-body experience, but they now returned. Simultaneously, I took my full first breath of fresh air after returning to earth. It was a rebirth. I was coughing and gasping for air like a newborn. I could move my eyes, my eye lids, and slightly move my neck around while trying to rise up onto all fours.

I could feel my body again, despite the fact that most parts were numb and freezing cold. I felt my feet, my legs, and my lungs. I felt my face on the ground and the weight of my body. As I consciously recognized my physical parts and all of their functions, I suddenly felt the enormous pain within my chest. That pain was still there. It was strong. It's what made my soul leave my body in the first place, and for a fraction of a second, I felt how easily it could happen again. My soul considered abandoning this broken, painful body just to feel the bliss again. But no, I had a mission now, I had orders. I felt empowered and I wouldn't miss the chance of facing life again. It is a beautiful planet, you know? My body felt broken by the pain, but I didn't want to die. I was excited. My will to live was much stronger after my spiritual experience. As I gained a greater realization of what was happening to me, I somehow found the strength to roll over and climb to my hands and knees.

I tried to get up, but my body was still too heavy. I needed more oxygen in my blood in order to fuel the machine. My breath was still very thin, like a clogged pipe. I felt weak, cold, and pale, but I knew I would be fine. I took a couple more breaths and focused all my efforts on the simple task of trying to stand. I made it to my knees again and got one foot on the ground. I then put my other foot down. I remember making the decision to do it; I visualized the kitchen door and with all my might, I got up. Standing, I walked in the direction of the house: one foot and then the other, step by step, inch by inch. I was not moving fast, but at least I was moving. I could feel my freezing, pale face and thought, *Damn, I'm in trouble this time.* I've always been prone to broken bones; falling from trees or off bikes, bleeding and getting stitched. I was used to emergency rooms, but this time I knew I had scored a big one.

Like a drunken man, I felt quite numb. I could hardly differentiate my left foot from my right. I had to fight through my lack of dexterity and balance to keep going, step by step, trying not to fall again. Wobbling, almost dragging myself, I reached the open door on the patio. As I entered the living room, I saw my grandmother sitting on the couch knitting. She looked at me, and I said, "Call an ambulance," before falling onto the couch. I was pale and cold, freezing, with very low blood pressure and labored breathing. I was tempted to close my eyes, but my gut told me not to. I continued to insist, "Call an ambulance."

We were in the countryside at the family farmhouse, which was a good ten miles from any main road. While beautiful and private, its location is not ideal if you are in need of emergency care. Once a huge plot of land, my great grandparents gave more and more of it away to their children and grandchildren. They used to own a bank, insurance companies, and an agro-business in South America. They eventually had eleven sons, and each one purchased pieces of land surrounding this home. Luckily for me, one of my aunts was a nurse and my grandmother immediately reached out to her.

As I was sitting on the couch trying to catch my breath, my aunt came running into the house along with the two cousins I had been riding dirt bikes with before. My grandmother kept suggesting that I should drink some water with sugar. *No time for that*, I thought. *I am in serious pain, I need an ambulance, not sugar water!* Upon first glance, my aunt said, "Hmmm ... he does not look good. Something is wrong." My uncle said, "Let's take him to the doctor in the village, and they'll tell us what is going on." So, the boys picked me up by, lifted me into the car, and drove me to see a doctor. Perhaps I was hallucinating, or perhaps it was my access to another dimension, but this was the moment I saw the Grim Reaper—*Death*, let's just say the word—out of the corner of my eye, standing between the house and the car. He stood looking, with his long black hood and sharp tool. Leaving the Grim Reaper behind was a bit of a reality check. In the back of my mind, I was thinking, *Shit ... death does exist. It comes, visits you, and slices your life away in a second. If he wants to take you, he might return without a warning the next time around.* It made me wonder how all of these characters came to be. Do we make mental projections of what we see as kids, or does someone draw them after a near-death experience?

I could hear my family wondering about my state of mind and body. They drove as fast as they could on a dirt road. My uncle was once a professional race car driver (and a good one, too), so speed was not a problem. My aunt kept making contact with me, saying, "Don't let go," or "Don't let your lights go off." She knew that if I wandered off I may not return. I felt safe. Love and care surrounded me, reminding me of why I wanted to live. And I did want to live! Not just because of moments like these, but because I felt the love keeping us all together. I could feel how much we valued each other, and how it mattered.

The four of us were zooming toward the clinic in good hands, but I was shaking, sweating, freezing, and in tremendous pain. Even so, I knew I would be ok. After all, I had just spoken with management (Entity) and had been given assignments for my next time on earth. I knew I was going to make it and I could fee His presence all the way. And so, I was enjoying the blissfulness of my experience, relaxing, and taking it all in.

The first time I relaxed, while lying by the garage, I believe that I allowed the release of Spirit from the damaged body so that it would no longer be in pain. I believe the desire to not feel pain with permission to release allowed the soul to leave the body, and consequently, resulted in death. It's funny to see how doctors or nurses know from experience that they must keep the patient engaged and conversational, or else the patient will die. Now, we know they don't die. It's just a release from the physical body because the other side feels no pain. I never fully felt the pain while I was apart from the body. I was busy in flight, chasing something new and unique, absorbing the knowledge of our non-physical side and looking for answers in a world above me. It was pure bliss!

It was a quick trip to the medical center. When we arrived, a long-time friend and family doctor was waiting for us. He looked at me and said, "Oh, boy," and then immediately ran some diagnostic tests to confirm what he already knew. As we waited for the results, he called an ambulance to take me from the medical center to the hospital. I saw people moving away and silence creeping in as the paramedics took over.

When I was placed in the ambulance, everything changed. It wasn't a familiar feeling anymore. Things suddenly seemed more professional, more detached, and everyone seemed more serious. It crossed my mind that this wasn't going to be simple. Apparently, I wasn't just getting an injection and then going home. This was only the beginning. Here, I clearly felt another fact of our existence. Arriving to a public place with mostly strangers in the room, they saw me as being in a life-and-death situation with little hope of survival. The scenario rapidly changed into a totally different composition. I saw and felt the power of assumption at the molecular level, the third level of mental projection; it was like a new room, new personalities and a new patient, me. I realized and felt what they could see and how their perceptions changed what was happening. The power of thought. When you change your perspective, the things around you change. And that was the moment I felt my vitality dropping again. Powerful stuff.

This led to a funny sequence of events that occurred between leaving the medical center and being loaded into the ambulance. The sun was brightly shining, and I was half unconscious and half awake. As I looked to the side, I caught a glimpse of a smiling priest who was clearly happy to not be signing up another customer. Again, I don't know if I was hallucinating (I am sure my body was releasing all kinds of chemicals to numb the pain within my chest) or if I still had access to other dimension, but I saw him, and it was an intriguing experience.

With this, I raised my awareness and consciously clung to life, intent on enjoying it the best I could, in any possible way. I resolved not to waste another moment ever again. Physical death is certain, and it will come without warning. Life is phenomenal, so enjoy it while it lasts.

As my chest and body were still aching terribly and barely functioning. I asked for painkillers, which no one wanted to provide to me because they suspected that I might have overdosed on drugs. This was clearly not the case since I hadn't touched drugs in four years. Still, I wasn't allowed any medication.

Once inside the ambulance, I had a second full-heart stop. I once again saw the light at the end of the tunnel, left my body, and once more experienced the feeling of amazing plenitude. Light was everywhere, and I started floating into an undefined space. I felt no pain, free of my body. All was peaceful again, and the all-knowing feeling and vibration returned. I was one with Spirit again, feeling the amazing bliss of non-physical being. But this time, shock pads brought me back. I didn't feel the defibrillator's shock, but I do remember the sudden switch between the spiritual world and my physical reality.

I rejoined my body and came to life again, gasping for air and opening my eyes. I will never forget the first face I saw—a paramedic with big eyes who was staring at me with a very serious look. Seeing me wake again, he smiled. I could see in his face that he wasn't sure if I'd make it. His uncertainty was evident. I was happy to see him, but I was getting angry, too. Not only had he brought me back from my blissful state of plenitude in the Spirit zone to my uncomfortable physical body, but he also refused to give me anything for the pain that I experienced.

I remember thinking, *Make up your mind. Am I going? Am I staying? Either way, I don't need this pain.* So, after I caught my breath and opened my eyes, I sternly looked at him and said, "Give me the painkillers." I guess he knew I was serious and that I wasn't overdosing because he asked me if I had taken any drugs. Of course, I hadn't. "No, not in the last four years," I replied.

At this point, I heard my uncle's voice talking to the paramedics. I realized they had stopped the ambulance on the side of the road to administer the life-saving procedures. I think they figured there was no point in racing to the hospital if I was going to flatline en route. They spoke to my uncle, he shouted back at them and the ambulance took off once more to the hospital at a high rate of speed. After a few seconds I became a bit more relaxed. I believe this time they dosed with medication as the pain became bearable. I was able to let myself go, trusting the process and allowing the experts to keep me alive.

Our next stop was the hospital, which took us about twenty minutes to arrive. Thank God the facility was equipped with state-of-the-art machinery for cardiovascular intervention.

However, no qualified technicians were on hand to operate the machines. The bad news kept coming.

I started struggling with the pain again, becoming inpatient and angry. I could see and feel the uninterested vibe around me. I still had difficulty breathing, I was aching, and I had to do something to turn this situation around. My memories are vague, but I was told I had another heart stop. I also remember a mix of vibrational states and mental spaces. They realized I wasn't safe yet and was in a volatile state of health. I remember asking for more painkillers to which they responded by telling me to relax. I could barely breathe and had no motor functions. I had a green light from the Source and felt that *human thinking* was blocking my survival.

I was then strapped to another stretcher and moved back into the ambulance to be taken to a different hospital, this one focusing on heart issues. It was a thirty-minute trip to Lisbon. I was in a *I don't care anymore* state of mind, so the trip was easier and with less pain. I was literally in a *fuck it* mood about any possible outcome, so long as the pain was gone. I think I dozed off from the medication. I remember occasionally trying to talk with the paramedics about what was happening. They kept telling me to relax, and that we'd be at the emergency room soon.

We arrived at the emergency room entrance, the paramedics got ready to take me out of the ambulance. I noticed hospital personnel were awaiting my arrival. They were all lined up, ready to work. Some family walked with the doctors and nurses to take me in. I remember being rushed into the ER, presumably for surgery to heal my broken ticker. Nurses were everywhere, and several doctors walked around giving instructions. They asked me how I was feeling. As I tried to respond the anesthesia kicked in—*boom*—I was flying with the fairies.

I woke up several times during surgery to ask what was going on. They replied, "Go back to sleep. Relax, everything will be okay!" I followed their advice and did so even as I felt foreign objects inside my flesh. I completely switched off, allowing myself to sleep. I remember waking up after surgery relieved that my heart functioned correctly. I could feel a refreshing influx of blood moving though my entire body as if it was completely dehydrated and thirsting for the vital red juice. I could feel it running through my veins, like a fresh and vibrant energizing fluid. It was great, I felt happy again. I knew things were moving in the right direction. And in that moment, I allowed myself to slip away back into the stars, dabbling in the conversation I just had with my non-physical friends, knowing that I would soon put my new heart to work.

Chapter 7

Getting on with Life

Time to keep true to the light, to love, and to honest intention.

My body and soul were finally joined together again after a period of time that almost made them strangers. I awoke after surgery to a blissful feeling of a life in plenitude, but this time in the flesh. I had a tremendous feeling of gratitude for all the people involved on my rescue. I was grateful for everyone who played a crucial part in keeping me alive and putting me back together. I wondered if they knew what was happening in the non-physical world while they were performing their work.

The nurses around me were amazing, and the entire staff was used to dealing with heart patients. After all, this was the cardiology hospital. They were kind, and demonstrated tremendous respect for survivors, smiling upon eye contact. Each would often say, "Not everyone survives heart attacks, you know. Not everyone comes back." Others would ask with big shiny eyes, "Have you seen Him, did He speak to you?" To which I would smile back in admiration, pleased to know I wasn't the only one. I knew Who she was referring to, which made me wonder, who was that Entity God? Was it a messenger? Was he an interpreter? I do know today that All That Is can express itself in many ways, using its magnificent and infallible Universal Intelligence through many energy points of access, Spirits, and entities of the non-physical. The staff had likely been dealing with these types of issues for many years, becoming experts in their respective roles as fixers of the broken-hearted and the undead.

For a few days post-surgery, I couldn't move much. Besides that, I was still in awe digesting what I'd been through. With it all very present, I was content to be alone at times. The doctors managed that very well as they recommended rest and staying put. They told me to rest. I was relaxed. I was in peace. I was grateful to be alive. I was also lucky to have visitors; it was incredible to have occasional visits from close friends and family. At some point, after many *aha* moments, I even felt like I needed change my birthdate from its original day to the day I was reborn and resurrected after surgery. I felt a rebirth inside of me. In the end, I didn't do it, but September 14 will always be a special day for me.

I was eventually moved from the ICU to a recovery room where I was closely monitored for another two weeks. The medical professionals performed more and more exams on me, regularly checking my heart to ensure I didn't suffer any kind of infection relapse. They were concerned with the potential for *arrhythmias*, an irregular heartbeat. Soon enough, they allowed me to move around and eventually to do some exercise. I also stopped smoking. After the event, I didn't even remember that I had been a smoker in the first place.

I was getting strong and eventually the day came when they said I could leave. They explained that my heart was 69 percent functional, that "it had been hard one" and I had a big scar to prove it. While a great deal of damage had occurred in the muscle, doctors told me I could live a good life with solid care and lots of love. To be honest, I didn't care much about that. I knew what I could do and how much I wanted to do those things. No one could stop me from living my life.

The doctor also shared I had survived because I had practiced an advanced yoga technique in which you slow down your heartbeat to a very low rate. This was news to me, as I had never practiced yoga in my life! When practicing, the body survives with low oxygen intake, maintaining vital organs. They were stunned I even made it, but the scar on my upper chest was the evidence that I had suffered a catastrophic heart attack. My heart stopped three times, and the doctors couldn't understand how I even walked to the house after the initial attack. They were very surprised that I had made it this far. I didn't know what to tell them except, "Thank you very much." After this note from the doctors, I made it a priority to investigate and start practicing yoga whenever I could. Not only was I curious about it since they said it saved my life, but I also wanted to use it as a tool for a healthier life in the future.

A Fraternity of Enlightenment

Because they were such experienced doctors and nurses with cardio-survivors, they shared with me a few thoughts that survivors often have in common. "They're enlightened, you know. They have spoken with God," an older nurse told me. "They always know what to do; you don't need to tell them anything," she told my close family members who came to pick me up. "He now knows exactly what he wants and when he wants it," she continued. "You have to let him be. It's time to leave him in peace," the main cardiologist said.

Their words offered me some solace as I saw they understood my extraordinary experience. It was a comfort not to be alone on this remarkable journey. I discovered many records of extraordinary encounters with the Spirit world, enlightening experiences that a number of people before me enjoyed. I felt safe and reassured. After a few days in conversation with one of the nurses, when asked again about my conversation with God (I had recounted most of it to her), she was happy and very connected to it. She felt it, she knew about it, and from her perspective, that *was* God. I smiled and nodded back in love with the acknowledgement and support. Today I see it as the means the Supreme Intelligence finds to communicate with us on our departing day. We go through a transitional stage in an intermediate dimension to prepare us for the change. Yes, you can call it God speaking with you through that Spirit. Maybe that Entity was my guide, maybe he has many functions in the afterlife plane besides interviewing me or assessing my next route. There's a lot of information to process and even more to be discovered and decoded from the blocks of information given that day. Still today I have aha moments of clarity.

I spoke with many survivors while in the hospital. At least three other survivors shared a similar journey; we all felt that we knew each other, and we were in peace. Our experience of life was through a different window, on another dimension. It was an amazing view; each of us respected one another, as we could see Spirit represented in our enlightened faces. We were on a mission now, liberated and guilt free.

The old nurse was right. I not only felt enlightened, but I also saw others who'd been through the same procedure as enlightened beings. I could see Spirit in them. Unconditional love; I guess we bring it with us. Once you've experienced the light, it can't be ignored. We take it with us, as its presence is the most benign source and can be trusted, a direction of peace, easiness, compassion, love, and light.

I left the hospital with a huge smile on my face. I believed my gratefulness was contagious. *I'm happy because I'm alive, so others must be happy too. I have another chance to live, to enjoy life with my loved ones, and to find new people to love.* Love became the major fuel in me. Gratitude felt inevitable, as everything was perfect, and I had the opportunity to see it. *I am grateful to have a chance to be alive and to love,* I thought and felt.

I said goodbyes to the hospital staff and left through the underground garage. My mum was driving, and I was in the passenger seat. We arrived at the first red light and stopped. We were on one of the busiest avenues in town with multiple lanes. As the light turned green and we moved through the intersection,

I noticed people running about their days and had an immediate and strong reaction to the chaos. I said to my mother, "I can't live like this."

It was too much; traffic, people rushing around, cars honking, policemen everywhere, beggars on the sidewalk, and children following behind their parents. There was a heavy energy in the air. It didn't feel right at all. My mother looked at me, confused. This was normal to her, city life at its best. She asked, "What you mean? Are you in pain? Are you okay? Do you want to go back to the hospital?" I said, "No, Mum, I'm okay, but I won't live my life like this anymore."

I continued on in a very calm voice, "We're not meant to live like this, in pain, struggling and suffering on earth. We're better, and we're supposed to live better, in peace, in communion with our planet, respecting Earth's gifts and ways. Life is a gift to be enjoyed, but none of these people are living with enjoyment." Not to sound arrogant, but I could see clearly what everyone was missing, what everyone was forgetting or refusing to live by. They should all know that we're not supposed to live under this type of pressure, that we're supposed to live a life of abundance and plenitude, respecting our planet, as it lives within each of us.

This life is a gift, yet the majority are not grateful for it. We're living in a magical, beautiful place and we should live accordingly. The earth has a way of expanding, developing life, and we're part of it. So, with that in mind, why do we stress ourselves every single moment of the day? We should not, we *must* not. My mum went on about how people have to work and support themselves. She clearly thought I was still high from the painkillers, so I decided to keep to myself and we carried on with the trip.

I couldn't believe what I felt by observing such frenzy and confusion. I knew I wasn't going to stay here, in this setting, this way of life, subjected to the circumstances of this vicious cycle. Maybe it's this country, maybe it's just this city, this society, or maybe it's only our attitude and how we view things. But I knew I'd live by other concepts. I'd have to leave the country and go in search of myself, in search of my way to experience this planet according to the teachings I'd just received. At the very least, I knew I was going to live my own life according to clarity I received from above. I knew it would be difficult to explain these concepts to people who struggle with issues that are not worthy of their attention. I felt it immediately after the incident. Each time I tried to explain the messages I got from an Entity in space, well, you can guess what the typical reaction was. I wanted to shake them and wake them up, but as the old saying goes: "You can lead a horse to water, but you can't make him drink." I decided it was up to me, and that message was being proven right already. I had to just take care of myself first, and let the results speak for themselves.

I had to stick around town for the first year after my release from the hospital, as the doctors suggested I stay close so they could monitor my health condition. They were obviously concerned I might have another episode. Twenty-seven years old is considered a young age for heart issues. I'm usually good at following directions (if I believe in them), so I took their advice. I stayed home because it felt right to do so. I had been given the opportunity to connect within, take time for myself, and recover from this event, so I took advantage of it. I sensed the need to nurture and take care of my body, and it was good to see family.

During this period, I made a great deal of improvements in my lifestyle, beginning with my diet. I visited an alternative nutritionist. Though not approved by conventional medicine, the approach he practiced had more than three thousand years of proven results in Asia. He moved to Portugal after years of studying and practicing in Asia to teach and spread the knowledge and benefits to others.

He was brilliant, and we soon engaged in a fertile connection; I could feel positive changes arising. He looked at the lines on the palm of my hand and could literally see into my soul, describing my experiences and traits. He went on to say he could see in my hands that I would have another heart issue in a near future, likely a few years down the road. This proved to be unsettling, but informative, nonetheless.

He then looked into my eyes and came to various conclusions based on their colors and shapes. He offered me incredible knowledge about the consequences of what we eat, think, and believe, and I was in awe. I still practice some of it.

He then went on and on about what I could and couldn't eat, explaining that different foods are good for one person's anatomy, yet the same food can cause completely different results in others. He shared with me how tomatoes can be healthy for me but make someone else fat. He prescribed me a tailor-made macrobiotic food lifestyle and outlined daily rituals, including singing a happy song out loud to start my day and resting with hot water towels draped over my shoulders, which felt like a hug from the universe. He suggested many other non-traditional practices that made all the difference in raising one's well-being. As you may have guessed, a heart attack is directly related to our own notions of love and our experiences feeling love. It's our heart after all, right? I would basically have to watch out for my emotions and feelings. "Take good care of your heart; you love too much," he said.

Cleaning Up from the Inside

I immediately followed this new diet of fish and vegetables, lots of fruit, lots of algae and organic products. I was an avid smoker before the incident, a pack a day of Marlboro Reds, but I kicked the habit after the heart attack as it was not serving me at all. It was easy to stop smoking. It was not even a question to consider it again. It's a nasty habit. My two weeks in the hospital worked magic on my attitude toward unhealthy practices. It didn't even cross my mind to smoke or to hurt myself in any way after such an incredible experience with the Supreme Intelligence. We are incredible beings, so how could I consciously harm myself now?

I took time to walk at least an hour each day, which I did religiously. It was a great pleasure, not only because I was living on a beautiful countryside farm but also because our black Labrador named Secas would tag along each day. He loved the walk, as dogs do, and was always so happy to see me. He would jump around or fetch a tree branch and drag it around for miles. He embodied pure gratitude for life and interaction; I guess this is what dogs do. He loved to be alive and to share this daily experience with me.

I couldn't yet work but I had an insatiable appetite for knowledge, so I took this opportunity to learn and read. My imagination was fired up, connected to the spiritual out-of-body experience; visualizing the dimension, idealizing for desired realities for my next experience. I kept connecting with the Entity, not only during my regular and daily meditations but also during my walks, digesting the information and planning how to use it. All I had to do was focus on my breathing, take deep long breaths (this has been my norm since the event), and within seconds He would be in my presence. I would savor every second of blissful energy; my questions would be clarified, and my positions reinforced. We had regular chats about nature, family, and life in general. Sometimes I would voice what I was receiving from his presence during long walks in the woods, cementing the things I had learned while out of body. Other times I vocalized the Entity's messages to other people. It would shock them a bit and they slowly ignored it, but I knew I was talking truth. Later, I understood this to be an activity called channeling. It was new to me, and it was priceless. Connecting to Spirit was a tremendous source of love, peace, and knowledge.

Even the thought of the word *work* was revolting to me, I knew I had to search within and figure out what I wanted to do. This period was very fruitful; my mind didn't stop simply because my body needed rest. I was grateful to be at my grandmother's house during this peaceful rehabilitation period. She wanted company in her home, a home that was too big just for one, and

I enjoyed being there. Family visited often and I enjoyed the time we spent supporting one another.

I had a new attitude toward life. Spirit had been extremely influential and impactful, and it inhabited all of my body and consciousness. The message was so important and incredibly positive that I kept reliving it, feeling it, and holding it with me to carry forward.

I wanted to share it with people. I wanted them to know that we all can live in plenitude, peace, and abundance, and that we can all be what we want to be, with ease. I wanted others to know it's all about being happy at the present moment. I wanted them to know it's easy to be happy. But for now, I was still trying to create my own connection with reality. I needed some ground rules to work with. I needed some results to prove I was fit for duty. I was exploring the psychic experience in a desire to remain connected with entities, but people around me were expecting me to return to their reality. I had a new reality—a reality where I can be happy now.

I was based in a very spiritual world in line with understanding and with being. I was in such a light space that walking almost felt like floating. No baggage, just being. Mostly, I was keeping my vibration as high as the clouds while still inhabiting my physical body. Why should I have to lose such a fantastic feeling, that perfect vibration, just to inhabit a body? The Spirit flies higher than the mind can ever imagine, but we can maintain this connection with Higher Self while grounded. It didn't have to stop. It was easy to keep the Spirit within my soul as long as I kept the joy, and trust me, I experienced a lot of joy roaming these beautiful fields with Secas.

Not everyone is keen on listening to spiritual experiences, so I kept it mostly to myself. I was a survivor who was more alive than ever. The time with my grandmother on the farm was an important part of my own personal growth and development, as it formed foundations for the new paths I would journey on in the future.

Chapter 8

From Fantasy to Reality

*When channeling, Spirit is brought through and the
creation of a new reality becomes clear.*

One of the main goals since my awakening was to search for and find all the possible information and knowledge regarding out-of-body or near-death experiences. This included various so-called practices of witches and angels, or anything revolving around the Spiritual world, not discarding religion. I didn't pay much attention to religion, since it has gone way off track from the initial teachings. The information is there, but it is distorted and can lead to misjudgments. When you are touched the way I was, you are reminded of our inherent sense of wonder and discovery, with new doors being opened. Finding answers and learning more about the soul, the spiritual world, consciousness, and the non-physical becomes a lifelong journey. I was thirsty for this information, and for any records that could further enlighten me about events like mine, since I knew I was not alone in my experience.

As my intuition was elevated, identifying charlatans or scammers was easy, and I could feel those that knew the truth. The vibe is different, it's dimensional. Removing all skepticism, I went to an astrologist (who was mind-blowingly accurate), an Asian medicines practitioner, and a psychic reader, and I learnt to be an energy healer for myself and others. I had a great deal of information from traditional medicine, but it covered only a small aspect of my overall experience; it covered the physical manifestation side, but I wanted to know more from the level of consciousness. I needed more because I had seen more. I'd left the body and the physical world to deal with the energy that gets us here, so the norm no longer answered my questions. I wanted to hear from someone who knew about these matters through experience and endless study, or at least, someone who could recognize what I had without doubting. Bringing subjects typically understood as fantasy into the world of reality is indeed a thing, it's just not for everyone.

One teacher got herself into a trance state to initiate a regression in an attempt to see into my soul and learn more about me. This was a funny place: she literally had a crystal ball in front of her, the decorations in the room were out of a movie, and the entire density in the air was different. She shared with me that my soul had travelled through many others on earth. She mentioned I had been during the Middle Ages a wizard or sorcerer, a mystical man who made magic potions to ingest and give to others. He gathered crowds and talked about these medicinal cures until he was chased and eventually killed by speaking out against the ruling system. Perhaps not coincidentally, one of my favorite comic characters is Panoramix, a wizard who made a strong potion for Obelix so that he could defeat the Romans with superhuman powers.

My soul's other mentioned life was as a mid-1920s actress, but I didn't learn much about her other than the fact that she was a bohemian alcoholic. We quickly moved on to my life in the here and now. She shared messages from the other side, which made total sense regarding my experience. She knew exactly who I was and where I was in life and what I needed to hear in order to carry on.

The teacher said I had a massive force opposing me, opposing every one of my ascending movements. The force was constantly putting me in check, allowing me to go down and explore the darkness, but never to explore the light. It kept me from joy, love, and consequently, from academic or professional achievements. I was literally housing my own arch nemesis; it was co-existing within me. The only reason, according to her, I had such great opposition was because I had such great light, a great gift inside of me that I needed to share and bring forth. I could do amazing things and had huge potential and abilities, but I couldn't quit. I was a very strong channel for light, and I would with Spirit's guidance. All made sense and reinforced my sense of crossing dimensions.

"With great power comes great responsibility," she reminded me. With the laws of physics that surround us, I had a great amount of work to do to overcome the obstacles and achieve success (happiness) in life. She encouraged me to work it all out, explore and evolve the bright side. I could keep the darkness in check and away.

Her words felt like a story of mysticism, of Spirits and dark lords, good and evil fighting for survival. However, I understood who was who, and that there's no good or bad, just different wishes. I knew what she was referring to, and it all made perfect sense. I had dreams of adding a system to the world that would change conditions from famine to abundance and free food, free housing, free education. I had dreams of peace and love, science and nature working together; but in my dreams I was called a lunatic and a dreamer, lost in utopian ideals that could never be achieved.

I knew that with organized planning one can work the fields for food, save the forests and rivers, and thrive without causing damage or pollution. The earth has everything we need to survive and evolve. It's been designed that way. Life, the Supreme Intelligence, wants us to evolve because no action can exist without a consequence. Plus, one could create a comfortable environment according to one's desires and ambitions. Some are born for art, some for humanitarian subjects, some for farming, and some for teaching, but being any of these things doesn't require us to destroy the other.

I regularly felt this urge, a duty to implement what, at the time, were revolutionary ideas. But in short time, I'd be put off and ridiculed by the opinions of others. I would feel and constantly see light bursting through me, just to let it fade by listening to others. I'm not blaming others who shut me off, rather, I'm acknowledging that I didn't gather the necessary strength at the time to ignore them and carry on my ideals. But that was then, and this is now! The psychic lady continued. "Communicate with the spirit world, as for guidance," she said. I would change this right now! I felt no need for approval from anyone but Spirit from this point. One aspect of immediate action needing change was my openness and trust in other people. I likely (and unfortunately) shared my ideas far too much with others before taking action. I know now that's a mistake, as you can only share your dreams with the few who believe in you, support you, and understand you.

She said constant opposition would be waiting for me during my next move, warning that I should keep watch. I had the creativity and imagination to accomplish it, to idealize and create my own path. Ignore this shadow and continue evolving.

The thought of this shadow guardian helped explain my tendencies for sadness and dark thoughts, the depressive states and destructive behaviors I'd manifested since the age of seven. How easily I used to quit and abandon any task when faced with opposition. I knew life could and should be easy, so when I faced something that required great effort, I believed nature was telling me, "Don't touch it; don't destroy it; it took me thousands of years to make that." I had an attitude of, "If it's hard, don't do it." So, I struggled with anything that required me to put in great effort. I believed things should be easy.

At some point, I developed a system where I required a sign from Spirit to know if I was following my intuition or my ego. I wanted to choose the right path. When I thought about something, I would do the exercise of choosing A or B before making a firm answer. You know when you stand too quickly and sometimes have a head rush, where you see stars or flashy white lights everywhere while you're a bit dizzy? I had a system that I developed while using substantial psychedelics in the 90s where a light would flash between myself and the backdrop landscape. As if you have a transparent screen between yourself and the person you're speaking with, and in that screen a small light would flash like a lie detector or a safety zone alarm panel.

For example, I might see a light, either green, red, white, or blueish purplish. Depending on the color of the light, as each color would have its own meaning, I would know what kind of forces or fields of action were at play. Then, I would understand the situation and make a better decision. This is a place in life where you know there are (invisible to the naked eye) forces at play at all times either we believe it or not. I've been a believer for many years. I've followed the lights since those days and have loved it every step of the way. Dogs, cats, bats, flies, and snakes, to name a few, can all see, hear, and smell things that we as humans cannot. But no one says we can't eventually start using those abilities or working with those dimensions. Yes, I know, you might not like this part or think I'm crazy, and that's okay!

Once the light would flash, I could feel the simultaneous change in the energies around the situation, opening new doors and possibilities to be unfolded. The best part is, I knew that I was not the only person seeing and working with the light system. I could feel non-physical acknowledgement of what was happening, reinforcing the choices I made. Yes, I always wanted to know and work with the unseen or unknown forces around us, and time has given them to me. I knew it was a perfect guiding system for a guy like me; a spontaneous, quick-thinking, emotional person. Remember, I used to follow the wind, the imagination, or whatever would catch my attention.

Green and red lights are the most common, and the white light is almost always covered or eclipsed by a black dot, trying to hide it but never strong enough to hide it completely. I could see the black dot rushing to try to cover the light. I knew if I saw a black dot rushing in on a thought, then there would be a bright, shining message of light in place. Purple light comes when I'm dealing with higher entities or Spirit principles of higher responsibility, and great care to be taken. Let's say the purple light involves dealing with Spirit, the ether and changing concepts of reality. I always thrived on the quest for the fabrics of our existence, and the Law of Attraction delivers. It's not a common subject, one would be best to not talk about this at Starbucks or during a marketing meeting. It's people like me who enjoy these conversations.

Trust Your Intuition

Intuition always gives you the right answers. But at the same time, the mind can be tricked. Your intellect can send you in a different direction, distancing you from your best self. Hence, it is important to trust in your intuition, your inner self is always correct. I always loved having my own light and color scheme guidance system to help me with decisions. I would see the light, match it with a feeling, and *bam!* I could decide right there what I would do and what I would believe. And the results were based on truth.

After a while, it was time to try Astrology and see what the fuss was all about. I wanted to see if there was any useful information related to out-of-body experiences, as they're focused on the physical objects around our planet but take into consideration their energies and influence on us. So, I booked the best-known astrologist in town. He mentioned details to me that no one else could have known. He seemed to know me better than anyone, and we had only met twenty minutes before. When I went to see him, besides the tremendous amount of information he held regarding all corners of my life, he also pointed out a similar feature on my chart. As a sailor, I understand how the position of celestial bodies can influence the weather and the emergence of moods within people. This, in turn, will influence their decision. The cause and effect rule would create new emotions and scenarios.

He helped me to understand which positions the sun, moon, regent planets, and stars were in at the time of my birth and how it develops along my experience. This was not your typical Sunday horoscope; it was the exact position of energy sources and their ripple effect throughout my life. I did my best to listen and learn, but in the end, I take everything according to my intuition. If it feels right, do it. If it feels wrong, leave it.

When it came to my current situation, he pointed out many of the same aspects that previous teachers had pointed out. He said, "You have a great quality, and the space and ability for great achievements, but you also have great opposition. There is a great obstruction in front of you, and this tiring fact might make you quit most of the time due to resistance." In this case he said the opposing forces were coming from my father and authority figures, which made sense, as I had been a rebel!

I couldn't believe it. How did the astrologist know that? He smiled and showed me the charts and drawings. It was all Greek to me. He went on to explain how strong the forces were and how beautiful and powerful I could be if I focused on exploring the light. But I would have to be assertive, strong, and dedicated to following my intuition. I must never quit. I am sure this applies to everyone alive, but I guess I needed to hear it.

So far, the information I was seeking and finding matched the information I had from above. All the feedback pointed in the same direction and explained the same facts. This was enough for me to start planning my move forward in life. I needed to do more physiotherapy, recover my full health, and get on with it. Oh, and I needed cash. I'd need to find some of the green stuff so that I could move forward.

Through each lesson learned or each teacher I spent time with, it was all coming together. The information from each sector of life was completing the picture of what had been described by Spirit and reinforced by my out-of-body experience. As the information I was gathering complemented my previous understanding, I was cementing and creating a new reality for myself. It proved to be an awakening to a new life dimension of love, belief, and positive expectation independent of background. I now had the foundation for this new approach to life. I was excited, eager to move forward, and was totally fearless for the first time in my life. I was in my own heart, in charge of my own actions, and I didn't owe an explanation to anyone. I finally could just be, do, and eventually have anything and everything I desired. This was a phenomenal feeling and very refreshing to me. The world was mine for the creating, and for the taking.

Chapter 9

Detachment

*Being ethereal, spiritual, and energetic beings is our
first nature.*

It was now time to honor yoga. I wanted to fine-tune the
practice that had apparently saved my life. While I was
doing everything I could to heal my body, I was also trying
to gather information on my out-of-body experience. Through
yogic meditation, not only did I gain my mind back from the
masses, but I also found awareness of my spiritual energy
field, which was perfect for the mind/body connection. I did
so by using a friend's guesthouse with a beautiful setting in a
pine-tree-filled forest area with a fantastic view of the Atlantic
Ocean. An instructor would come there to perform yoga classes
with incense and typical sounds of healing. Taking the experience to incredible and immensely gratifying energetic places

was both relaxing and inspiring. I attended classes every other day and then practiced on my own once I had learned enough of the basics.

It was an amazing experience. I was enjoying the tremendous benefits of yoga, and it proved to be a great stress reliever. It helped me with discipline and self-esteem and allowed me to focus on personal development. The results proved extremely beneficial. I sensed a tremendous improvement over time in many aspects of my life.

Yoga is a regenerative practice, I totally recommend it. It can help you relax and connect to your Spirit guide regardless of your age or stage in life. It's always a benefit. It boosted meditation and intuition to incredibly new levels of insight and peace of mind. I was better able to focus, center myself, and connect with nature.

Not only that, but the obvious benefits of the regular stretching and exercise are also evident in your posture, agility, and strength. Yoga makes you feel fresh, youthful, and grateful. Your subconscious thoughts manifest more quickly. I found that yoga brings numerous benefits and pleasures, raising vibration levels over long periods of time.

My priority at that time was to search for my passion, for fulfillment in activity by trying out new experiences and possibilities. I wanted to create a future self that would live in joy and plenitude, thriving at levels the human condition has never experienced. I had learned that only I could change my experience in life, and I was accomplishing it with my thinking. Time was precious as I was looking to reformulate what I wanted to experience in my second chance.

While that might sound selfish, I knew I had to take steps to heal my body and develop my mind, and that was best accomplished without distractions. I had just survived a life-and-death situation and had been confronted with the fact that when we transition to the other side, we go alone. And it's not what we accumulated that matters, but how much joy we experienced. It was time for *me* now. Plus, how can you be good to someone else if you're not in a good place yourself? Put yourself first and everything else will follow.

I was ready for it. I was alive, with a strong heartbeat and lungs that could draw air. My mind was clear and as sharp as ever, giving me the feeling that I had the world at my feet and could do whatever I wanted through my creative abilities. How could I have missed it all of these years? Breathe, feel good, meditate, create, accept, and receive! Everything was clear now.

On the spiritual side, I'd come closer to my heart center, with all of my meditations providing me extra awareness of how to cooperate with the natural, universal forces at play. Following the direction of my mentors, I practiced detachment from material things, from mental habits, from old memories, and basically from anything that was not serving me or helping me achieve the best version of myself. I was only keeping and exploring the good side of life, focusing on love and beauty, accepting the perfection of our habitat The mission was to drop anything that didn't bring me joy, as positivity would be my most precious fuel to propel me towards the realization of my dreams.

Another positive change I recognized during this time was a shift in my eating habits. I cooked my own macrobiotic food in a special way. I loved my food and appreciated fresh vegetables, almost talking aloud with them to share my gratitude for the benefits they provided. This was an intentional way of living, and I achieved it by removing all the negative practices.

And that's the whole point. I almost killed my body (I actually did, but came back!) with my previous behaviors, so it was not only obvious but also easy to accept the need to change. It was very peaceful, and every meal was a pleasurable experience filled with fresh flavors and colorful dishes. My physical appearance changed within weeks. My metabolism improved, and my sleeping habits and general well-being were at 100 percent all day, every day. My energy level was through the roof and I could connect with the Entity easier and more frequently. My vibrational radius was enormous, and I could feel at peace in any situation. We are what we eat, energetically and mentally.

I also nurtured my intellect. As I had more free time, I was constantly studying the Law of Attraction and avidly reading about personal development and understanding how my health had escaped me. Every day, I would regularly walk through nature in peaceful bliss, meditating as I walked, channeling the Entity, the Spirit Guide, and so much joy was being taken in. I take a drive to swim in the ocean and would meditate. Activities that boosted my day and helped me to progress through recovery. I loved the fact that I was in charge, consciously progressing with intention. I could see the daily improvements as I wondered how far, and in how many directions I could expand my knowledge and abilities. I was thrilled and knew this was only the beginning.

On one of these days of replenishment I received a call from a cousin. She is a very special person, very spiritual and very understanding. She is someone I've always admired and who's had a great impact on me. All of her life, she's been very much involved in alternative practices to fully explore the mind and body, trusting that's the way to repair mankind's issues at the core. I used to see her as a modern age fairy godmother as she's very mystical.

She lived in a magnificent 400-year-old palace with small patches of organic vegetables, fountains, and a beautiful and impressive collection of metal bells. These bells each had a different vibration, and if you hit one with a soft hammer and turned your back, you could feel the vibration and sound of the bell working through your body and your soul. Some bells helped to develop roots, some were to expand your mind, and others enhanced your soul and connected it to the Source. Others were simply for relaxation.

The natural sounds of the bells were designed to produce the right frequency of vibration that would activate certain reactions in your body, consequently developing positive effects for you. Walking through that garden of bells, which unlocked, expanded, or reinforced human experience, was gratifying and enriching. I loved it and would repeatedly go there to cleanse and learn. I would walk to the house and meditate. Being able to get inside this place was a privilege, like a bubble of parallel reality with no limits.

So, she called me one day and said, "You *have* to come meet this guy. I have him here for two weeks doing a phenomenal workshop with fantastic information. You just have to see this." I was obviously very excited as she always had great resources, and this teaching seemed in line with my interests. However, I told her, "I have no cash at all. I can't afford it." But she insisted, "Ask someone. You can't miss this. Just ask your mum or something." I didn't want to ask anyone to borrow money. I'd left the hospital one year ago and wasn't working. I was basically living off of the charity of my family until I got back on my feet, so I didn't want to ask for money for courses.

We hung up the phone, and I carried on with my daily tasks. Just a few minutes later, she called again: "I spoke to your mum, and she agreed to pay for your course. You'll sleep in my house and attend the course. I'll see you then. Bye!" I was stoked, humbled, and very grateful. I really wanted to move forward, grow, get independent, and be rich, powerful, and happy. I didn't know how to act, so I just accepted it with pleasure and promised to give my best to this opportunity. *I must make the most of it*, I thought with a smile on my face.

I felt a great vibration from this event, fantastic energy from the 400-year-old palace and its enchanted gardens. It seemed that it could be a quantum leap in my life. The timing couldn't have been better. I was free, open-minded, and willing to embrace something new. I believed it was important for me to complete this workshop.

I called my mum to thank her for this gift, promising to pay her back once I could. She said it was the right thing to do and knew it was worth it to spend the money. After the phone call, I felt very confident, believing this would be a life-changing moment. And it was. Excitement, faith, and inspired action can turn dreams into reality.

Changing Your Inner Dialogue

The course was a Neuro-Linguistic Programing (NLP) workshop for self-development and life coaching. It focused on how to achieve, be, and do whatever you wanted in life and then eventually help others to do the same. The main principle of learning to speak is to use words correctly. It's to change your inner dialogue and self-talk while recognizing the power of what we say and think at any stage in our lives. When one learns to control both inner dialogue and audible speech, they can create the life they want. Words are powerful.

Both my mother and cousin were right, as this was all I wanted and needed. The universe had delivered it to my door, and all I had to do was to accept it, allow it into my life experience, make the most of it, and take action. I would learn to work on this new craft and create the space and intention to receive results.

This turned out to be one of the best experiences of my life. The main coach was fantastic, a cardiologist who had changed careers to become a life coach and NLP practitioner. He worked everywhere from New York to Sao Paulo, and throughout Europe. He was brilliant to the core and devoted to the art of self-improvement. He began the workshop discussing how speech and vocabulary are not only the roots of our subconscious mind, but they also create a positive ripple effect in our lives. Words have energy, and that energy will dictate our thoughts and, consequently, our actions and lives.

That was only the beginning, and already we were in awe of the power of speech. Over the course of an amazing week-long session, he showed us how to create the life we wanted, from thought to planning and from action to receiving. He shared how to choose a destination and explained the importance of setting it. It doesn't matter how you start, as long as you start. We all must have a goal in life, otherwise life will just pass us by.

We practiced his techniques, meditated, exercised in teams, and then wrote down our goals, wishes, and dreams. We participated with an open heart, and a lot of writing. One of the most crucial exercises was to state our goals in detail, writing and feeling every aspect of them. We outlined our objectives and lifestyle choices in a variety of areas, from building companies to creating millions of dollars to having successful relationships, careers, and hobbies. We also wrote about what type of person we wanted to become, physically and intellectually.

We wrote and envisioned our goals for one year out, three years out, five years out, and ten years down the road. It was a fantastic exercise of previewing our achievements and was very stimulating as it engaged our imagination and helped us identify who we want to be, what we stand for, what we believe in. It helped us understand what we want from our life, how we want to live, and what message or legacy we want to leave behind. This was all covered in the first section of the course, and we devoted the rest of our days to amazing and intense exercises on imagining and feeling, which solidified our achievements.

We were searching for the feeling and the sensation of having it already. The joy in the room was gigantic and gratifying as all of us envisioned ourselves with our dreams as a reality. Act as if you have it already, be the winner you want to be, be happy now for having what you want, and the universe will bring it to you. It almost felt like hypnosis, since we were fully committed to being our future self, eyes closed, walking into the life we choose. It was a time capsule and we were in it—amazing!

It was great fun, as we were all very loose and trusted the process. We'd travel in time to the exact moment of achieving what we wanted, like buying a dream mansion, driving a Ferrari, sailing the world on a yacht, or skiing in Switzerland. We'd write down the goal, focus our love on it, and then travel in Spirit to live the experience. Rotating though the room from person to person gave us great support and we collectively believed in each other's the dreams. The entire sequence of experiences was so mind-blowing and realistic that it was quite emotional. Another surprising and beneficial side effect of this exercise was to see how among twelve different people, each of us had different desires! So immediately, the feeling of non-competition and abundance of possibility filled in the room.

With love and in Spirit, thinking our desires from conception to fulfilment brings them into reality. I tapped into abilities that I never knew I had. We made good connections after deep dives into each other's goals, masterminding our dreams, and literally co-creating a life reality that fit our tastes. The people who I kept in touch with from this course have all manifested their desires!

I went home super motivated after the event, regularly practicing my homework and following up on the teachings of co-creation with immense clarity. On the side, I continued to study these amazing materials. I was fascinated, mostly with the feeling of designing my own life. I had considered becoming a coach myself, just to dig deep into self-development of the hidden powers of the brain, mind, and NLP.

Fast forward five and then ten years, when I returned home from sailing the world, I'd read my notes from that coaching course. To my satisfaction, I realized that I had achieved 100 percent of the goals I outlined. Even more, I've overcome my goals to gain even higher ground, so much better and higher than I ever imagined. It was a mind-blowing experience.

Right around this time, the powerful hit movie *The Secret* by Rhonda Byrne was just released and spreading like wildfire. At night, we'd watch the movie in groups in someone's living room, sometimes during parties, in the afternoon, or even at random times when someone would press play or bring it about in conversation. I feel grateful to have been introduced to all of its wonders. The first time I saw the movie I intuitively felt that I already knew it by heart. Various sections helped me to think differently. The most satisfying aspect for me was the excitement of the participants and knowing there was a movement focused on a *thoughts become things* lifestyle, as it was very similar to the teachings I received from the Entity!

On the other hand, though the concept of quantum physics was totally new to me at the time, it rang a familiar bell as memories from the out of body experience kicked in. I had seen life energy molecules in trees, stones, wind, and sand when I was out. The subject was way out there, but it had some familiarity to it, and it was gratifying to know that scientists were working on the connection between thoughts and matter. Metaphysics. The more I studied, the more I felt my place.

On the practical side, the to-do list of exercises outlined in *The Secret* matched with the exercises I'd been practicing since I left the hospital. I felt supported by a synchronicity in everything that mattered to me, involved in a thought wave of creative power designing a new world. Empowered by this alignment, I could *feel* things instead of just seeing them. I would feel the energies of people, places, forests, and animals. I knew everything was communicating with me, so the level of attention I gave to something was related to the energy I would feel in it. I knew I was energy and I had seen everything else as energy; with the explanation in quantum physics, that door opened even further.

One of my favorite references, for obvious reasons, was the "Miracle Man" Morris Goodman. He was the example of something I intuitively knew since childhood, as I've always healed quickly and thoroughly. An adventurer from a young age, I used to hurt myself while playing with sticks, climbing trees, or riding bicycles. I would get cuts and scratches and would bleed and break bones more than the average child, but I always recovered well and fast. I realized from an early age that this was so simply because I wanted it to be.

As a very active kid, I wanted to get well quickly so I could go out and play again. Everyone else I knew would take longer to heal. I wanted to heal, and so I would heal. I knew I would be well soon, and so it was. I would *intend* it. I'd give a command to my body: get fixed. And it would be so. From a young age, I believed we have the power within ourselves to control the cells of our own body if we focus and devote time to it, using the power of intention to bring healing. Health is a mental state. I learned that from experience, even with my friends. I'd tell them, "I heal quickly." And I would! Today, I heal quickly.

There was a documentary playing around at the time, *The Silence of the Monks*, in which a group of monks used their focus of meditation directed toward a small section of their garden where vegetables were growing. On the side, they kept another small section of the garden where they didn't focus their meditation. They produced a more visible and larger growth in the vegetables they focused on compared to those in the conventionally farmed part of the garden. Not only did the vegetables grow to extraordinary sizes, but they would do so at a much faster rate. It was amazing to see what could happen when a small group of people focused their positive energies and intention. As I watched, I had that feeling of *I knew it* once again.

It's funny that when we wonder about things and use our imagination, we can feel the truth within each thought or ideas. Then, someone shows up with the exact vision we had within our imagination. We intuitively know some facts as truth, even if they haven't been backed by science or with any practical experience. We just know it. And I believe that's how dreamers bring innovation into reality. They see something that is not yet here and bring it into the physical world. I love these aspects, as they makes me think of space travel and interplanetary trips, instant teleportation, the ability to levitate, invisibility, or even longevity—our constant health with instant regenerative cells.

By acknowledging the fact that we as humans have the power to do things like manipulate the growth of plants and work in the quantum mechanics of our existence, we gain an exciting opportunity to become responsible for new abilities as we bring them into reality. If we can use the power of our minds to grow plants, how can we not be responsible for other events that involve the same kind of molecular manipulation? Remember, it's all made from the same thing: energy and thoughts are energy, so we can use them!

Yes, I know it sounds sci-fi, but so did the idea of putting a man on the moon, or even the thought of flying in the first place. I believe we need to activate other abilities in order to perfect the theory that if we have an idea, it's because it has happened already within a parallel reality. If every memory or every thought, which are all energy, exist since its inception, then it proves the theory. If we think of levitation, maybe it's happening in a parallel reality on a similar planet not too far from us, but the memory exists. Their facts as thoughts travel through space and what we get here is an idea, a suspicion. This is happening for a reason. I love this.

NLP, coaching, and *The Secret* just following a near-death experience all came into my life at the perfect time, and collectively turned out to be a major turning point. The following months were decisive for determining my next twelve years, as I've used those techniques to accomplish what I desired.

Although the movie was spectacular and enlightening in every way, what really opened my imagination was a hard copy of *The Secret*. I continuously read it, back and forth, studying its messages and choosing pages at random to revisit. I studied it any time I could. Paragraph after paragraph, I read and thought about the similar life paths that clicked for me.

The biggest excitement I was taking away from this was that most teachers had turned their life around, mostly after thirty or forty years of age; they'd been broke on the streets, and all of them turned it around, becoming very successful in their choices as a result of focused and intentional thinking. That was an inspiration. If they can do it, so can I.

Think, feel joy, ask and it's given.

Chapter 10

Powerful Realizations

Feeling, believing, and accepting the power of mind over matter!

With continued development of both body and mind, I progressively recognized substantial differences and improvements in my life. Most importantly was how this new information was proving to be true, reinforcing all that the Spirit Guide told me on my visit. Everything was clear and true. Following his advice, I saw the results and therefore continued to shape myself in life regardless of the opinion of others.

I was happier, more active and peaceful, I was eating well and exercising, always eager for more knowledge and to find the practices that would better my future. I had already learned so much about how the body and mind evolve. I was thriving, and I had no intention of stopping or even slowing down. I was

savoring the moment, enjoying every pleası
bliss.

One day after a Pilates class, I met a very nice and ⌐
young lady who shared her story with me. She survived a ι⌐
rible illness at the age of twenty-three. She fought a strong
battle, took the bumps, and survived. We had something
very strong in common in that we were both given a second
chance on the planet. We were calm; we knew we had survived because we wanted to live, and we were excited to know
the value of this gift.

After chatting for some time, she offered me her own copy of
The Body Mirror System: Anything Can Be Healed, by Sir Martin
Brofman. The book offers a fantastic journey toward healing
through the energy we allow in our body from our thoughts. It
also details the pathway of specific emotions that trigger symptoms within our body and how to heal them.

Everything Has a Cure

Health wise, everything has a beginning, and everything has
a cure. Mr. Brofman outlines the way our body works energetically and how the cycle of our thoughts, and consequently
our emotions, dictate the vibration level of the energy running
through us. This strong combination of thought and feeling
dictates the growth, shape, and health of our physical body, its
organs, and its functional ability. Basically, any physical symptom is a consequence of an emotional conflict, which creates a
different energy connection in the pathways of our body. This
is directly related to our self-talk. Not to mention our general

⸝hape, which is directly dictated by our beliefs, not necessarily through what you eat. Mind over matter, always.

The book explores our inner connection to the seven main *chakras* (there are a total of 114 in the human body), which are the swirling wheels of energy that correspond to massive nerve centers in the body. Each of the seven chakras contains bundles of nerves connected to major organs and systems of our body and to our psychological, emotional, and spiritual states of being. We also have 72,000 *nadis,* or energy channels, through which vital energy flows. And obviously, as the magnets that we are, we will attract matching vibrational beings and events into our life experience.

Since everything is energy and energy never rests, it's very important to keep our seven primary chakras cleared, aligned, and fluid. Connections derived from bad feelings or bad thoughts will close the channels, weakening the chakras, creating a congestion of energy and stopping it from flowing freely. If the negative thoughts persist, they will eventually create tension that manifests in symptoms.

As every one of the seven chakras correspond to different areas of our lives, it's easy to identify the area of our life that is worrying us or creating conflict or hard feelings by considering the affected section of the body. Once you identify the cause for the emotional stress, then you can deal with it and work through it, causing the healing to happen and the symptoms to disappear.

Everything is comprised of energy, including our thoughts and feelings. Our thoughts develop into feelings, which also dictate our resonance, state of energy, and how we feel. Brofman explains it very simply: bad feelings make you sick; good feelings lead you to health. Easy!

This was one more lesson about the amazing connection between thoughts and physical manifestations, or mind over matter. It's important to understand this relationship, as it gives total responsibility to each individual. For me, it was a missing piece of the puzzle. Chakras offer a map to identify the potential source of any anomaly in our body and the means to immediately fix it. It was a fantastic study, to say the least. I totally recommend *The Body Mirror System: Anything Can Be Healed*, so that you can have the right guidance.

In one section of the book, Brofman outlines the emotional causes of common diseases. No illness develops from just one factor. They are always the result of a sequence of events and mental or emotional persistence. For example, he says cancer develops in people who have many emotional peaks with steep and repetitive highs and lows. As for the heart chakra, the one that got me kneeled to the source, here are some tips transcribed from the book itself on what it's associated with:

- Parts of the Body: The heart and the blood circulatory system. The cardio plexus as well as the lungs and the entire chest area.

- Endocrine gland: Thymus, controlling the immune system.

- Sense: Sense of touch, in its aspect of relating to the person inside the body. Distinct from the orange chakra, which is more about the sensation one feels from skin contact. Hugging is therefore a heart chakra activity.

When one hugs, one is aware of what the person inside the other body feels, and they are aware of what you feel inside your body. Sensitivity about being touched indicates heart chakra sensitivity.

- Consciousness: Perception of Love, relationships (relating) with persons close to your heart. For example, your partner, siblings, parents, or children. Difficulty with breathing, or with the lungs (the organs of air) indicates tension in the heart chakra. A person's relationship with air reflects their relationship with love. For example, AIDS is a problem with the person's perceptions of love, since it is the immune system which is affected. The person feels that their lifestyle separates them from those they love, often because of societal judgement.

- Element: Air

In this style of very clear and effective texts, the book takes you through a fantastic recognition of your body and the power to heal yourself, from Everything. Thank you, Mr. Brofman.

Anything related to the heart chakra can create a domino effect. For example, complications can arise from our notion of love, what it means to be loved, and how loved we feel. Anything negative in that force field can create heart problems. So, it is important to deal with all thoughts and feelings as they come. Don't be shy or afraid no matter how much discomfort you feel. Feelings are temporary, and avoiding worry will help you avoid disease. Remember to keep your health first because there's not much left without it.

Brofman also teaches how to raise one's level of energy to stay healthy and balanced. Between meditations and specific exercises, one can manipulate energy and heal others as well. Shortly after reading the book, I started to regularly control my energy field. I raised my meditations to higher levels and found deeper Zen states. I got answers to my questions and experienced a state of bliss very close to that of my encounter with my Spirit Guide. That was the goal, to experience heaven on earth.

At the same time I began practicing this, I started surfing with my friends. "It makes you feel amazing," they had said, and that was what I was looking for—things that made me feel amazing. I tried it and loved it. I found an unbelievable connection to the natural elements, to the wind, sun, and water. I not only enjoyed the physical exercise but also the fantastic feeling of riding a wave. Working with natural forces brings something out in us, helping us to focus as we master balance and movement while flowing with the natural rhythm of the earth. Basically, surfing is standing on a floating board on a moving mass of water on a flying rock that's moving through the solar system. The focus required in surfing connects me to the source of all things, to all that is.

During the periods of high levels of energy and vibrations from surfing, I started having some amazing experiences. I found that the shape, size, and form of the waves coming my way would change according to my focus and attention to them. It may be a bit farfetched, but I believe we have the power to manipulate and organize water molecules our by using our focused intention on the rhythm and the earth's momentum to shape the waves. I'd stay in the water waiting for the waves, and when I focused, they'd come where, when, and how I'd visualized them with only a fraction of a second delay. It was truly incredible! I felt as if I was adding to the supply of nature.

When returning to dry land after surfing, you feel an enhanced connection. You're relaxed, body, mind, and soul, with a new perspective. You're in a high vibration for the next few hours, and everything you're facing seems easy. Nothing can really worry you. That's the main benefit of surfing; the other is that your body shapes to perfection.

Again, I had attracted one more source of joy with surfing. Plenitude is within as you run through the waves. It is freeing and empowering. I loved it. I could restore my body faster and in a more complete way through this natural energy. Once I'd re-energized myself with exercise and meditation, I could feel the energy within the palm of my hands. I'd then use this energy to heal myself and others—by request only—with a method similar to *reiki*. We do have incredible powers which can be used to create the life we so desire.

To complement my time in the ocean, I created the habit of meditating on mountaintops while enjoying great views of the horizon and beautiful forests. I loved sitting by trees with their fantastic energy, feeling pure love. Other times I'd simply meditate on the beach and use the relaxing rhythm of the waves as a guide to Zen. I'd be living parallel realities in my imagination, very uplifting, leading me to create new roots for growth in possible scenarios. Part of the reason of my heart attack had been a feeling of losing home, as I wasn't allowed in the house I grew up in. I had lost the biggest relationship of my life, which was with my family. I felt that I had lost my roots and identity, so creating new ones in naturally inspired beautiful and imaginary places was a daily practice, grounding myself in the creation of new foundations.

It was a rebirth with the awareness of the previous life. I felt like a virgin of sorts, so I craved information from the earth, the planet, and the ether—not from people. I was finding that I needed something new and natural. I'd had enough of people and their emotional charges at that time, so I ran away looking for inspirational and natural places on earth where I could receive it straight from the source. I was going within.

I wanted to connect, to feel my origin and update my purpose on this floating rock. I had clear indications and directions from the Supreme Entity—my Spirit Guide, my Mentor—but I still wanted to feel more of the relationship that connects the earth to the cosmos. Since we always find what we want when we look with intention, I found nature to be an amazing source of clean, pure energy, where life exists peacefully in perfect symbiosis. I found the food I had been craving.

I knew my health depended on me being in a good vibrational state, and if I was, results would follow. I wasn't wasting any time, and I appreciated when others followed suit. It took a while to get the message across, but I was blunt about it and my colleagues and friends seemed to get the point. I was practicing daily gratitude for all the good things in life, even for simply the ability to breathe on the earth's playground. I was grateful for the awareness of my powers as a co-creator of my reality, using thought, strong emotions, and desires to fuel my actions.

I'd elevate myself so high in states of well-being so that I could feel the same Energy that I had when up in the clouds meeting with the Supreme Entity. I'd tap into these high vibrations with ease, using unconditional love and feeling the plenitude required to feel worthy of my best life, to attract it, letting the universe know this is the new me. I was deeply rooted with the earth's resonance, feeding from natural energies like water, plants, and beautiful areas while uniting my aligned chakras with the beam of white light emanating from the stars in the cosmos. I'd visualize an energy light beam from the universe passing through my Zenith, through me, and toward the center of the earth. My roots.

This powerful connection would put me in the driver's seat as I shifted to my best life on earth. This was a part of what the Entity had told me; it was part of the to-do list and his teachings about life. He explained how to be in charge of myself, how to take control and give myself a happy life. He taught me to have experiences, excitement, and happiness. And I did, knowing that I am part of the Source just as he is (and as we all are), following his direction, trusting and learning his ways, acting in joy and bliss.

In searching for connection with others with the same knowledge, I found many in similar vibrations and many souls with similar intention for this present lifetime, which is fantastic, to create a place of love, joy, light, and happiness. I was not alone anymore! Little by little, I've been moving toward this goal, gaining the necessary self-confidence to start working on my visions and desires. As a teenager, I was a kid for the masses, trying to satisfy others, or at least the greatest number of people

I could. If I made a crowd happy, I felt better and accepted. Now, I was the only person I wanted to please.

To keep my anxiety at bay when I was young, I ran around trying to please my family, then trying to please the rich and powerful, then trying to please the poor, then trying to please my country, then my girlfriend, and so on. But trying to please others before taking care of myself led to a dead end, literally. I realized pleasing others without meeting my own needs was not the way. Actually, pleasing others is not the way period, though it does feels nice to surprise loved ones with kind gestures! If I please myself, develop myself and be good to myself, I will meet, connect or attract those with similar viewpoints that will be already pleased with the encounter. There is no need for effort. Life is just beautiful. I was thrilled when introduced to this new way of life because it was so inspirational. Putting myself first by creating my best self offered me a fantastic life. And then yes, I could treat my girlfriend, my mom, or my friends with something I knew would make them smile. Then, it's possible to be nice to others!

If and when we create the space and focus loving energy on it, we can get what we want out of life. I love this phenomenon, this gimmick given to us in our root game rules! But we will, perhaps, have to discover this potential at a later stage when mankind might be more in agreement and have the necessary advancements to believe in it. As in any other areas of life, we add and transform what is given to us, and if we believe in our powerful abilities to create worlds, we can adjust life to meet our vision. If we can connect and control or manipulate energy with our thinking, it must be according to the electromagnetic composition of all matter. It must be energetically connected through the space between movable matter and ourselves using our intention. Consciousness before matter, that's the real power.

All in all, I've met people and practitioners, teachers and guides, and sources of information from different schools of life all pointing in one direction. We are energy; we become what we think about, and the happier we are, the happier and higher our thoughts and vibrations will be. This will attract a matching reality to our emotional state. All of these teachings lead to us to this truth: we can happily create our reality. But we must dedicate time and thought to it. As long as we focus on being happy, feeling well, and being in a good vibration, we can control our experience. That's what we all want. And I wonder, why isn't this subject taught in school?

Chapter 11

Daily Practices

*How do I keep my vibration high? I continue to dream
and being happy in the moment!*

I'd like to touch base on a few bullet points to review the practices that boosted my self-development and purpose. These are disciplined actions to empower and project the ideal life. Here are the main ideals I was working with:

- Bliss and Joy are our natural states, born rights, and only our thinking disturbs this.

- We can do whatever we want with our lives; we are free. We can be whoever we wish to be, with no limitations.

- Intuitively following joy, excitement, and happiness are my best guides (without knowingly hurting anyone).

- We have within us the power to change and create as we want with desire, intention, and assumption. Tune in and use it.

- Our life is supposed to be lived joyously, in an abundant state of being, in plenitude, in bliss, in love. It's a birthright, and a natural state. We're not here for suffering or to struggle.

- Imagination is my best friend. It's a powerful tool in the creation of life. All I need is imagination through thought and visualization.

- Find something you love doing in life and follow it! Imagine that you're already doing it and feeling its joy. That's the fuel to make it happen.

- It's okay to change. The fact that you've been a teacher for the last fifteen years shouldn't stop you from becoming an art dealer or sculptor today. Who you become depends on who you want to be.

- You don't owe anything to anyone, and you don't need permission from anyone to be who you want to be. The past is just that—the past.

- Others can also be, do, and have whatever they want and desire. Allowing them to do so is allowing you to.

- Meditate, connect with who you really are, let intuition be your guide; trust and become.

- People who matter will come to us, and we'll know who they are. It will be clear who to stick with and who not to stick with.

- Love is the magic ingredient; I use it all the time.

- Be happy now. You're alive, and, being here is a fantastic gift!
- We never really die, our soul is eternal and constantly evolving. Get over it. Don't take life so seriously; be happy! We only change form and dimensions.

At this point in my life I was writing in detail my dream life, reviewing it, and breaking it down into sections and areas of experience, and it was working!

Decisions

Making decisions quickly became a good practice, as doing so clears the way, allowing things to move forward. Wait a minute, think about them with intention, feel what is the best option, and do it. What can go wrong? Usually, we instinctively know what is the right thing to do, so trust your gut and do it. If it proves to be wrong, decide again on the opposite. Problem solved, and you didn't waste anyone's time. If it's from the gut with information, usually it's correct.

As time progressed, I'd been through a few weeklong jobs, doing as my Spirit guide told me to, experimenting with new things and taking risks in order to find something I really liked. I tried gardening, working with cars, landscaping, and even art—anything to make money for my next jump.

I had quit being an artist after only selling a copy instead of many pieces of my own! Being an artist was great; I loved the feeling. However, I wanted something substantial. I wanted more money for my time, more value, and making copies of other people's art was not the way! So, I moved on.

My next business venture was a gardening company that allowed me to work in people's private gardens. Some were big projects, some were just lawn mowing, and others took interesting turns. I'd trim big trees into beautiful shapes, plant exotic species, and reorganize people's gardens leaving a signature. One project took place at a 200-year-old house. It was more like palace from an old family of dukes and duchesses. I've always had a crush on royal environments. It's a passion. The big castles, the beautiful palaces, the large fireplaces and huge properties, lakes and gardens. I think I like the detail and grandeur of it. Also, the princesses ... ah ... they fascinate me, but that might not make me unique at all. Who doesn't like a princess? Who wouldn't love to meet one, let alone marry one!

What a pleasure it was to visit this palace. I'd stop and gaze at the whole place. I could hear the horses and chariots driving by in my mind and imagine the people doing traditional activities in different sections of the property. It was a sort of a time travel for me. I love when my mind and feelings take off like that, either into the past or into the future. It makes me believe that everything exists at the same time in different dimensions, and that time is only an illusion. I love it. Hence the question, where are the memories stored, especially if we can see and listen to the lives of past times?

After gardening for a good few months, I stopped when I had too many clients and realized I would need to expand the business, invest, and get more hands. I was getting tired from doing heavy gardening for weeks in a row for several months, so I decided it was not for me. Tools away! Great grounding, though most of my time revolved around beautiful sand and dirt, and planting close to 800 trees!

Getting Closer to the Truth

The next activity would reveal itself to be a real eye-opener. To some extent, they were all eye-opening, but this one was special. I decided to go to Brazil and work on a coffee and soya plantation at some large properties from one side of the family's elder generation. One of my cousins had lived there for decades running the business and was very successful. I asked him for a job and mentoring, as I wanted to leave the country. He knew of my process being aware of all my stages until being years in recovery, and now recovering from a massive heart attack. He kindly received me in his penthouse in Salvador da Bahia, Brazil, and took me for a relaxing weekend before dropping me in the deep bush.

It was incredible, and I had one of the best experiences of my life. I was not only the traveling through a foreign and different country that was so great, but the entire experience of the contrast of the local lifestyle. I've seen giant anacondas, large crocodiles, mammoth spiders, and frogs the size of a pineapple. I rode horses at sunrise to take a herd of 300 cows across the property, which is a full-day activity. I managed the team of workers on the fields to grow and harvest the coffee and worked closely with specialists who blended coffee mixes for new buyers to export. They held meetings on what type of coffee the clients were looking for—sweet, hard, strong, light, flavored, you name it—and then they would make a blend. I was growing in the coffee business and learning a lot. I loved it.

This position was developed for three huge farms, or *fazendas* in Brazilian Portuguese, producing coffee, soya, cotton, sugarcane, cattle, and high-level cattle breeding in auctions for reproduction. This took me to beautiful locations with breathtaking landscapes. It was very interesting, and it helped to open my mind to new horizons. I had that satisfying feeling of gratitude for the large number of opportunities that presented themselves to me as soon as I left my comfort zone. Immediately, I had new business ideas and lifelong plans. They were different every day, and so with gratitude I embraced them and enjoyed the expansion and mental activity. That was the purpose of the trip, to broaden my horizons. I had cleared the old and now there was space for the new. It was time to stretch and grow.

While living and exploring the region in large wild sections of forest, I met indigenous Amazon tribes that lived in lush green areas with crocodiles and large, color-changing iguanas, parrots, and the biggest variety of tropical fruit I've ever seen. This farm was in the southern section of the Amazon forest populated with the remaining indigenous tribes who have lived with the same methods for centuries. The place was full of life; fountains of joy, abundant fruit, and fresh clean water everywhere. Any day, at any time, you could pick up fruit from a tree or bush—mangos, acai, passionfruit, and an entirely new local spectrum of fruit. I saw the heat of the summer and the floods of the winter and how the landscape would change, and how the animal life would adapt to it. Dry areas would be flooded and transformed into lakes, water streams transformed into rivers where we could fish, make a fire, and cook the fresh catch for lunch. It was amazing, a lesson on the versatility and abundance given to us by this beautiful planet in a coexisting, perfect balance. The earth gives everything we need. The Amazon rainforest is a treasure we must protect, not only for its variety and daily work of being the lungs of the planet, but for the lessons it gives us. It was bliss! Ramifications of powerful nature expression are growing on a daily rate. A lush, abundant, and perfect symbiotic relationship. The planet showing off what it has for us.

Time went by and I realized I needed more culture, technology, and sophistication. The beauty of experimentation is that you're always winning, because even when you realize that a situation is not what you really want, you can move closer to the things you actually desire. Plus, you gain practical experience, memories, and the acquaintances made along the way. Traveling is a great medicine.

It is a conscious decision to take control and give myself the best life. I see it first, I live the role I want next year today. Imagination is the key and the vibrational point of that scene is the lock. Together, they have opened the experience of my life that I desire, and it depends only on me.

With this method I gave myself beautiful loving relationships; great sexual experiences, fantastic events and parties, met incredible people and tried exciting sporting activities. I'd tick bucket list events; I'd create episodes in my mind with expectations and desires, and then meet them, creating my reality. When I suspected they would soon be manifesting, I'd take action with faith and the courage to enjoy them and live them to the fullest. Realizing that we can die at any moment was the biggest gift I received that allowed me to really start living.

With this, I became more specific. I knew what I wanted, so I started seeing myself living in the easiness that I desired for myself and for others whom I could influence either directly or indirectly. There was plenty of money, millions for everyone, we'd be living in stylish beach houses, surfing daily, eating healthy, I was driving supercars (all of my favorites), living onboard my own sailing yacht, meeting interesting people, and dating a beautiful girl—a girl who was interesting and had character, was respectful, kind and trustworthy—maybe the love of my life! I was attending high end ceremonies in great company, going into palaces and castles, artsy environments and involved in life-changing projects, including cinema, art, and ecology with performance and innovation. I envisioned the best life I could create for myself.

Basically, taking life with a smile and asking, "why not?" I'd wonder and focus on how it made me feel special and alive, engraving in my subconscious mind the new person I was, in the scriptures of the universe, so that the quantum mechanics of the Universal Laws of physics could begin working on it, making it happen, allowing me to go from thought to reality. Lucid dreaming, I call it, the creation process. I want it!

My inner voice knew that I was enough and that I deserved it. Time to play!

One of the side effects I earned after the out of body experience was that I could export myself up to the skies again, beyond the clouds, among the stars and look at the Earth with all my possible timelines, and then I'd choose to send myself back to the one I wanted. In this case and period of time, I wanted to be a 100-million-dollar lottery winner! And I could see myself being it, really! And It felt great!

One of my favorite teachers, Bashar, repeatedly states: "Everything already exists now in the universe. You are the one that needs to shift into the vibration of the reality that you prefer." And so it is!

This was music to my ears, as it was the same message I got from the Entity up there. So, I'd exercise basking in the feeling of having received one hundred and eighty million dollars! At the time, this was a recurring max prize given at the European Lottery. I'd fantasize about what I would do after earning all that money! I accepted that this would be the system; this would be my choice, the process I had to go through in life. I had to feel my way into the life of my dreams and not leave it to circumstance, and I had to do it guilt-free. The only thing missing now was a kind of service or activity that I would play with in order to create some funds to start over. Funnily, this had been part of the message from my Spirit Guide: *try new things, have fun doing it, carry on, and don't look back!*

My new self-image was now that of a successful guy that was doing great in life. I just didn't yet know what thing I'd done that rewarded me with such abundance. Should I worry? No! Should I care? No! All I had to do was go forward believing that it happened already, and in the meantime, keep experimenting with new flavors until I find my favorite! Rhonda Byrne (and many others) said it in *The Secret*: "Feel as if you have it already, now." Whatever it is you wish to have or wish to be, live your life as if your wish is already fulfilled. Those words made the book credible to me as it matched what my Spirit Guide told me: "You are a loved, perfect, happy, a joyously powerful creative being." And if that's who I am at the end of the journey, that's who I can be now! I can be happy now, joyous, and I can have fun; I can be the person I want to be, because we are it already. And get this—the reason *The Secret* resonated with me was, as with the Entity, that our natural state is of perfection and joy. Mental activities make us deviate from it, and focus brings us back to joy again. But we *are* joy already, and in life when we chase things, people or events, it's because we believe it will make us feel better again. Feel joy *now*! Be the joy now and the universe must give you a place where joy happens, because that's how it is. Cause and effect! We are already bliss, so if you allow it, you are basically telling the universe that you already have what makes you happy! And the universe gives!

I had chosen to be happy and successful now, because it was different than my past experience. So now, I'd like to make a difference. In my self-image I'm a multimillionaire bestselling author whose books have been adapted into blockbuster Hollywood films. I even play a cameo role in one film, acting alongside Hollywood royalty. I'm involved in reforestation projects and ocean protection and reef farms! I also do public speaking at events where I demonstrate my channeling abilities. I love the idea of being invited to speak! I have a channeling community from Spiritual Guides, but I keep that private as well! I love this process of dreaming!

When people asked me what it was like to experience and survive a heart attack, my answer was, "I won the lottery! I feel like I won the jackpot!" The sheer fact of understanding what it is to have an earthly life experience and be aware of it was such a tremendous gift, I felt as if I already had everything one could ever ask for. Being alive and kicking was the biggest gift I ever received, and I knew it. So yes! I do feel like a millionaire already; when you feel that your life is being taken away, and this is only a place to explore and have fun with it, you realize how valuable and exciting it is to be alive! Yes, it feels like $110 million being given back to you when you realize you can come back and play! The happiness and gratitude I experienced for being alive again were higher than anything physical, any car, house, job, or even achievements. It's the thrill and joy of actually being here in a physical body, playing, and creating! *Thank you.*

I did want to continue trying new things and expanding, evolving, leaving a legacy, or just showing people how they can also be happy in this life experience. I wanted to show people how to not let their surroundings or circumstances make them quit, be unhappy, or feel less than their best versions. Initially I thought: *If I can help others by giving an example of what I have achieved, then first let me help myself and achieve my dreams!* And right there I just needed to find the starting point, my starting activity. That's what I wanted and what I was working for now. I would need an area of action to develop my gifts and open the door to receive all the good I desired.

I knew from experience that I would need to occupy my daily working hours with something I loved doing; it couldn't be just *work.* It had to be something I loved. I've tried having a job just for the sake of paying bills, and it wasn't for me. Now I knew I'd need an activity that would not only stimulate my intellect and give me pleasure, preferably both at the same time, but that would also contribute to the happiness of others, to the benefit of our planet, and to future generations. I knew that now, somehow, I had something to give, something to share. I had to deliver a message, channel this energy from my mentors, and it would be my pleasure and duty to do so. I had found a way to a happy life, and I believe millions of people can benefit from it too. Would it be through public speaking? Would it be a book or a motion picture? Was it the Spiritual Connection? Would it be simply being an example? The time for experimentalism was reaching an end, and I could feel it. I knew I had the answer in me. I just needed to tune in and let it flow, because the direction for my life was decided already: channeling abundance, plentitude, and bliss—Heaven on Earth.

Chapter 12

Manifesting Magic

Into the rich life.

Feeling. I know that's how I attracted this lifestyle with all the visualizing, vision boards, and meditations. I had felt it before. I had seen it in my mind's eye, loving it, dreaming with beautiful yachts and all the pleasures they bring. And now, sixteen years after my heart attack and for the last fifteen years, I have manifested many of my childhood dreams and more. Friends would say to me, "Whaaaat? You're so lucky! You're watching the Monaco Formula 1 Grand Prix while sleeping on a yacht with everything paid for!" Having lunch in Paris, sailing in St. Tropez, New York, or Dubai, diving in the Red Sea from a superyacht and sailing with fantastic people in the best events all became regular activities.

Not to mention, the growth of my career; I had become a captain on yachts, responsible for millions of dollars of property. If I'd get bored with a program or a yacht for not being my favorite cup of tea, I'd move on, attracting the next adventure. This time we'd set sail on a fantastic 200-foot modern classic schooner to sail around Europe, North America, the Caribbean, and Central America over the course of three years. I had written down this adventure on my life script seven years earlier, and it happened by the meter! I chose it, visualized it, felt it into existence—and that's one of the powers we have, the power of choice over our tomorrow! I was grateful for the teachings that allowed me to take charge and control my life experience on earth based on my desires. A later study would reveal that by changing my awareness and perception of life, I could switch to the other side of the bar, having this lifestyle as the customer and not the employee. With a click!

This was when I started using the Universal Laws more in-depth, as I wanted to change the time and money frequencies of my life experience. There are two ends to every stick. Now, I was holding the stick and I wanted to change which end I was holding.

As one of my favorite sayings goes, hardworking people tend to be lucky. I'd asked for the high life, and then I took action as soon as the opportunity presented itself. I jumped out of the comfort zone and said *yes* to life's challenges. Inspired action led to extraordinary results, from my deepest desires to their manifestation in real life, in the physical form, because I believed that I deserved it. Hence, I am drawing a fantastic life for myself once again at this time, because I know it works! I'm not afraid or ashamed to state it out loud to the universe or to anyone who asks with an honest heart. I deserve all the good that I desire. You should do the same as you read the following. Say it out loud:

> *I want a fantastic life. I want an exuberant life. I want a high-quality and luxurious life! I want abundance. I want love. I want plenitude. I want peace. I want an inspired life!*

Feel free to add anything you want. I do this exercise regularly, asking myself, *what do I really want?* Not what society expects me to want, or what my parents or my spouse or my brother or sister expect me to want—this is about *what I really want.* I love this!

But let's not forget, this was still a job. The laws don't make any mistakes, so maybe I forgot to be more specific and express that I'd like to try these things as the client of the yacht and not as staff. But at the end of the day, did it matter? I've visualized and wished for myself to experience the adventure, challenge in the high life, and the universe delivered it as a vibrational match of my excitement, of my visualization. The laws are precise; we get what we put out. I wanted to go diving in Belize; the Law of Attraction doesn't know if I was paying to do the dive or being paid to take someone diving. The fact was, I attracted that experience into my life according to my self-worth and vibrational density, which at the time involved the notion and feeling of needing a job. And that's the beauty; I can use my imagination, bring my vibration to a level and position of owning the yacht, or being invited to take part in these activities, and by the Law of Attraction, it comes to be. The work is with the inner self and the universe. It will deliver.

Let me clarify the saying above that I like. I consider working to be taking the time to feel yourself into the reality you want to experience. If we don't do that, we'll stay in the same place.

In this case, for two months I dove the whole of Belize and the beautiful wild islands of northern Honduras. It was a fantastic trip, with a fantastic group of people, visiting some beautiful corners of the earth in bliss! Sailing a beautiful $12 million yacht owned by some of the finest people of Germany to the most remote locations. Diving with sharks, swimming with turtles, and being with interesting people. I can laugh now as I know how it works, hence my advice for you is to be very specific in your desires, as they will manifest as you request them. Write them down in detail, put all your love into them, wishing well to all affected (if any) so that everybody gains with your growth and success, and you will only be a winner!

Still, I'm super happy, grateful, and proud of myself for manifesting those experiences. I've been having the time of my life in these years since I made the decision to accept joy and happiness, a righteous given. I loved it. I was living the rich man's life while working with something I truly loved and admired. I was fascinated with the large sailing yachts, the people, the exuberance, and the continuity. The type of luxury where the sheer quality of every detail mattered. One of my favorite aspects of this activity was and still is the ease of continuity. We never stopped, always moving from one fabulous place to another, finding out that this world is incredibly beautiful and perfect, with many tribes, activities, freedoms, and desires being manifested in the most diverse locations. Accepting and understanding the diversity of being. The symbiotic nature of its cycles is both humbling and mesmerizing at the same time. I love this planet and I love being here as part of it. We were always on the go for an adventure, a party, a dive site, a local monument, a lobster barbeque, or a thrilling sail to a wild island.

Money Does Matter

This was a big message to my subconscious mind: how easy it makes your life when you have money (correction, when you have a *lot* of money)! As I sailed these luxury yachts, I realized we were not in danger, nor did we experience anger due to hunger, and we never fought as a result of distress. We were giving and educating impoverished areas. We were helping the economy of remote locations. I'm not being arrogant or despising the poor. I was a hippie until my mid-twenties; I was an advocate of a money-free society. And do you know what? They exist, and anyone is free to join! There are currency-free cities and communities all over the world, and there are also economy-based societies and cities, which undoubtedly prevail. It's my choice to give it a go and try my talents on this one. It's my choice to use the financial and trade society to create the life I want. If you're an idiot, money will make you an even bigger idiot. But if you're a good person, money will only make you better; it's an enhancer, like drugs and alcohol.

We all have a choice. Every morning when we wake up, we can decide where to go and what to invest our next twenty-four hours in—maybe the rest of our lives, or at least as many days of it as we wish. We can always make a new decision and choose a new path. It's our time to be alive, and we're free to choose where and how to use it. I'm grateful for that!

Earth Has a Heartbeat

I like to be of service. I want to help those who can benefit from what I have to offer. I like peace on earth. I want everyone to have food and health and to live in happiness and make full use of these amazing powers which have been given to us. I want children to play freely in Gaza, Las Vegas, Vietnam, Syria, Madrid, Mumbai, Lebanon, Brazil, and Palestine—you name it. Everywhere in the world. I love peace; remember, I was a hippie. "Peace and love" is still my motto. I also believe I can only help others after I have helped myself.

What's happening in the world is strange, but I know it's a manifestation of our mixed vibrations. How can we call ourselves an evolved species, an intelligent species, yet kill each other like this? How can we kill our animals for pleasure, pollute, and destroy our home (earth) as if there were a Planet B? I used to believe it was the Law of Polarity working amongst the world population, that we needed positive and negative people to find balance. If so, would the only way to reduce the negative side be to reduce the positive side as well? Should we decrease positivity so that the negative will also decrease? Is that the *yin and yang* balance of the earth? If someone is extremely happy, does that mean someone else has to be extremely sad? Does one grow in exact proportion but in the opposite direction of the other like water displacement? I've thought about the Law of Polarity working in the planet, and I believe it might have been like that. But I also believe it was the age or dimension of the planet, and now entering a new density where we can truly all be happy, enlightened, feel well, and stop hurting and killing each other. Spiritual leaders have tried it all over Tibet, India, and many other populations where bliss, abundance, and plenitude are all given as a birthright of our souls being here. There is no need for suffering.

The earth has its own thriving energy, its own Love, I'd say, its own heartbeat. This is the *Schumann Resonance*, 7.83Hz. It's a vibration. Humans vibrate on an average of 6-8Hz, although some body parts reach as high as 13-17Hz and others as low as 3Hz resonance frequency (our thoughts can raise that up to a 70Hz frequency! Probably all we need to manipulate and form matter to manifest!) Earthing has many benefits as, which perhaps explains why we feel good when we connect to nature, in the forest, or on the beach. Earthing, (or grounding) refers to the discovery of benefits from walking barefoot outside, or sitting, working, or sleeping indoors while connected to inductive systems that transfer the Earth's electrons from the ground into the body. Earthing uses the Schumann Resonance to improve human health. By scavenging and neutralizing the free radicals in the body, antioxidants help to ease inflammation as well as cell and tissue damage. Earthing helps you to be grounded, energetic, youthful and clear! A perfect system indeed.

We all are an expression of thriving love energy, and there is no need for half of the population to be in a low vibration for the other half to be in a high vibration. We can all be in the same high vibration! This would actually help the earth to heal and the forests to grow better and faster.

A few fun facts: Other frequencies are said to have influence and power over the human body, soul, and spirit. 432Hz is said to be the natural frequency of the universe, giving us cosmic powers to heal ourselves. (This is not evidenced by science, however.) Why would the frequency of the cosmos heal us? Because that's where we come from, that's what we're made of—pure energy. It's our source of unlimited supply. Hence, no need for suffering and want; there's plenty for everyone! It makes sense to believe, but yet it's only considered speculation. Still, I have to wonder, is it only a coincidence that this frequency has been used for thousands of years by ancient musicians, healers, and spiritual practitioners?

528Hz—the love frequency—is said to resonate at the heart of everything, connecting your heart (your spiritual essence) to the spiraling reality of heaven and earth. This frequency was also used by ancient priests and healers. Math scientist Victor Showell describes 528 as fundamental to the ancient *Pi, Phi,* and *Golden Mean,* evident throughout natural design. As demonstrated in Shmuel Asher's book, *The Soul Revolution – Trinity of Humanity,* Showell and John Stuart Reid (a pioneer in acoustic research and cymatic measurements) have proven that 528 is essential to the sacred geometry of circles and spirals consistent with DNA structuring and hydrosonic restructuring.[1] The 528Hz frequency is associated with DNA repair!

---

[1] https://www.quora.com/What-are-the-benefits-of-listening-to-music-at-528-Hz. https://books.google.com/books?id=ofpuDwAAQBAJ&pg=PA112&lpg=PA112&dq=Showell+and+John+Stuar

Oddly enough, the 852Hz frequency, because it is directly connected to the principle of light, and light is a higher form of bioenergy, increases awareness and allows one to return to spiritual order. In the cellular process, 852Hz enables cells to transform themselves into a higher-level system, awakening Spirit! Into the fifth dimension we are!

Once again, the side of life that is not visible to the naked eye was being presented as the solution to my life, or at least to the better enjoyment of my life experience on earth. I've started to dig into the knowledge of the Universal Laws as I have enough proof that they work and are fundamental. I knew from meeting my Spirit Guide during my out-of-body experience that this was true; it mattered for me to believe, and the results demonstrated themselves. I knew firsthand and so I followed the thread of thought and schooling of those who had been through the same in order to find the same information and the same principles told to me by the Spirit Entity. Even though all information was coming from different channels, it originated at the same source—from the same energy of the Universal Consciousness surrounding us all, expanding in and through us.

Chapter 13

Repeating the Formula

The importance of maintaining the excitement!

Through the next years I continued to repeat the formula, jumping from sailing yacht to yacht job working as a captain or an officer, travelling and choosing where I wanted to sail next. I continued visiting new and unimaginable places around this globe, meeting incredible people, and enjoying the extravagant locations and cultures. I didn't really care about who was in charge because the real gift was the chance to get to know this planet and its people. I love it. The concept of working for someone in exchange for a salary was still very welcomed as I had no other idea in place. I was having fun, I enjoyed it tremendously, and I was earning more money than I ever had ever before. Life's fantastic.

I'd choose jobs depending on the travel destinations, the people involved, and the beauty and quality of the yacht itself. I love the design of these extravagant and innovative machines. Also, the sheer luxury and exclusivity was very attractive. As I said before, most people pay a fortune to be in this environment, and I was being paid to operate them. That alone gave me a daily boost of gratitude and excitement which enabled me to carry on working with and for these amazing personalities. Meeting renowned politicians who required FBI surveillance, Hollywood celebrities, royals, rock and roll legends and sports superstars—hanging out and taking them to dive or for an afternoon sail around Sardinia, yes, I was loving it.

As the bow sliced through the water like a hot knife through butter, I would often tilt my head toward the sun and remind myself that I was experiencing my old dreams in real life. My deepest desires were being fulfilled in so many ways.

Traveling was second nature, and it usually involved fancy destinations. I've regularly come back to Monaco, shopping and attending social gatherings, or just walking around and visiting the monuments, museums, theater, and cinema. Meeting friends for a coffee or a work lunch in St. Tropez became a regular outing and it was always exciting. Portofino, Mykonos, Santorini or the usual visits to Capri and the Amalfi Coast were always a pleasure and never a chore, even if I was still working! Driving exotic cars and ... did I mention extravagant, one-of-a-kind superyachts?

Every autumn I'd sail across the Atlantic Ocean and spend the winter in the warm Caribbean waters. I'd be working, mostly sailing, diving, and still had enough free time to explore and enjoy the culture, the people, and the scenery around me; beaches, mountains, and remarkable local historic buildings, not to mention the incredible food.

At that time, I had a steady relationship with an amazing girl, which made everything even better. We would rent a car to explore and travel inland to get to know the country we were visiting. Whether it would be an island or major continent, we'd mingle, cruise, and explore. Professionally, dreams kept coming true as we'd participate in the most exclusive superyacht regattas designed for the world's richest three percent to enjoy, and there I was in the middle of it, setting a spinnaker or trimming a sheet to round the mark. I have no doubt that it was a choice and a conscious decision to believe I deserved that brought me here from the moment I decided to allow it to be my experience. It's an amazing world we live in.

I sailed and lived onboard a $30 million sailing yacht where I could play the piano in my off time, eat from a $10K caviar box, and drink wine that cost more than a car. We cruised the Bahamas and visited the east coast of the United States in a very thorough fashion, partaking of the usual lobster barbeque, freshly caught from the ocean under us. Traveling the U.S. east coast was one of my favorites; up and down we sailed, stopping in every state to enjoy the local food, the people, and the sites. We held masquerade parties onboard and swam in the moonlight. And did I mention night diving? Oh yes, plenty of that, either to see the sharks sleeping or to explore an old famous shipwreck full of marine life. Again, I don't say this to brag, I say this because I had been sleeping in a car earlier in my life, in jail, or in the forest; my decision to experiment the good life brought me here. That's why I'm sharing this only with love for our time alive. Take it. Enjoy it. It's totally worth it, and it's free!

I'll never forget the moment we arrived in New York Harbor sailing on a 200-foot schooner called the *SY Germania Nova*, a replica of the *Germania*, a racing schooner from 1908. We sailed past the Statue of Liberty, up and down the Hudson river, and then docked to explore New York City. We spent an entire month in the Big Apple, sailing and enjoying its beauty. Besides visiting the monuments, we had the amazing gift of being invited to some of the best restaurants in the city and meeting celebrity influencers whose arrival required that FBI and Secret Service agents search and inspect the location of the visit—meaning our yacht—chatting with us for cooperation. This is straight-up Hollywood material, something you would see in a James Bond movie, and we were living it firsthand! I'm so happy and grateful, it's hard to explain. It proved again the value of daydreaming and the point of detachment and trusting. From the moment I focused on just being happy and not controlling anything, all my subconscious wishes were fueled with joy and brought into existence. I knew I had a great formula, and I didn't want to stop using it. I was loving life and living it fully!

We visited Savannah and the Forrest Gump bench, Charleston with its natural beauty, Annapolis and Baltimore for another great celebration (a prohibition-themed party onboard). We followed on to New York, Shelter Island and Sag Harbor, Newport and Providence, Boston, and then up Maine's beautiful coastline, one of my favorites.

On the way back, we hung out in Martha's Vineyard, meeting even more successful people, true American legends, and enjoyed the stunning beaches. Life was so incredible, and I knew it was sure to be true. I knew it, I felt it; I was visiting places I'd seen in childhood movies, meeting idols I had secretly dreamed of. All had been brought into reality because I allowed it to be. I allowed myself to shift from my previous lifestyle to one that I dreamed of, and it's ok to do so. We don't owe anything to anyone to stay where we are now. I was extremely happy to be alive, so the universe gave me reasons for that happiness. And on and on again, and it will keep giving as long as I keep accepting. I had to return to the notes from my coaching to find that I was working and sailing on the yacht that I had once described in detail all those years earlier. Everything happened just as I'd written it! Desires, wishes, ideas, and environments. This was the realization of magic, and it was happening to me.

My "Aha" Moment

This lifestyle could have continued for as long as I allowed it to. It's like they say, "Shoot for the moon, and if you miss, you'll land among the stars." I was happy. I had some money in the bank and I felt myself growing in all areas.

It wasn't until I visited Dubai that I had a real "aha" moment. That city had a profound impact on me, making me feel that I needed a change, an increase. I loved it there. The biggest impact on me came from a vision. There was nothing there, only sand. It began with an idea; a visionary imagination with passion to create a fabulous New World city with no baggage! No cultural paradigm! There was no history imposing heavy historical facts or traditions as an emotional or intellectual burden on us. The Arab culture obviously existed, but the urban city was a mix of visionaries and dreamers with a brand-new platform in which to start fresh, start something new, and I love that!

As a captain on a motor yacht based in a marina on the incredible manmade Palm Jumeirah island, I gazed at the shimmering skyline and felt like a pharaoh. This innovative and visionary city, with luxury quality all around, was very uplifting. I don't think a place should be judged based on its exterior factors only, but if any external influence is happening, let it be a positive and uplifting one! Dubai has that, and it made a great impact on me. The impact was not only due to its opulence, but also because many of the individuals I met there were in a contagious vibration mode of *dream a fresh dream*.

The people I met in Dubai were committed to their cause without wincing, and at the same time, embodied serenity and calmness imposed by the atmosphere the city emanates. Consciously dreaming, building, and stretching themselves, and they were winning! Inevitably, I had a reality check being surrounded by an ocean of opportunity into the life of entrepreneurship. There I was, giving my life for a salary, a paycheck at the end of the month. It didn't feel right anymore. It didn't seem to match my knowledge and experience. I felt worthy of much, much more, much better, and I knew that I could do otherwise.

Was driving yachts around beautiful places a bad job? No, not at all. It was great fun, and I met fantastic people and visited amazing places. However, from a Spiritual point of view, was it worth the price of my soul for my time on earth? Hell no! Did it serve a purpose, and was now the time to change? Yes! I'm a perfect spirit with a pure soul living in a physical body, and so are you. We are powerful creative beings. So why was I selling myself so short? It was just my awareness growing, I had overgrown my current activity. Now, I had a desire to change the way I live on the planet. I had a desire to change the area of exploration and growth, the way of interacting with love and with the earth. I had a change in me; experiences, dreams, love and ideas. I had to do something about it. My Spiritual self was here and calling for me.

Transformation Activation

Personal growth had become more important to me at this time than professional growth. I wanted a transformation. I wanted to use my soul's resources to their best ability, to help people, to enlighten the ones who needed to do what I had done—break out of the comfort zone and away from the fear of opinions to live a life on the exceptional and happy side. Suddenly, I knew I had to. I felt an immense need to grow, stretch, and serve for the good life of many others. What good would my transformational process be if I couldn't share it with others and help them enjoy life as well? I had to change!

Oddly, this period also coincided with reaching the end of the goal-achieving list I had created ten years earlier. I had reached the goals I set for myself for a ten-year plan, and we were now close to 11 years since *activation*, so it made sense that I would feel this excitement. I was eager to learn more and thirsty for a change in life. There was room for it now!

I went through my list, my notes from the coaching program, to find that I had accomplished all the goals (and more) that I had set out to accomplish in one, three, five, and ten years! In some cases, the detail was correct down to the color, size, and shape. The positions, the cruising, the process, had all been as I had described it to be. I knew it worked. I knew what I had done, and I loved it. I was loving the system we live in, and that could only bring more gratitude.

Coaching and NLP had worked wonders for me, and I knew it. Now, in a place of pure satisfaction with life and myself, I wanted to create a new direction. This time I would shoot for the moon!

More than ever, I wanted my deepest and wildest dreams to come true. Why not? After all, ten years had passed and I had lived what I chose to, so who was I to set any limits upon my next ten years if I have the gift of life? I'd give everything to myself. I deserve it. The universe deserves it, and anyone around me deserve it as well. If I'm my best self, I can only benefit the lives of those around me! It was time to get back to the drawing board and design a new life for myself. For now, I wanted to buy one of the houses on Palm Jumeirah by the yacht marina in Dubai. I wanted to buy my dream cars, a Ferrari and a Rolls Royce. I wanted to have a stunning, intelligent, caring, and progressive wife. I wanted Hollywood. I wanted to live in LA on my own sailing yacht, a good easy life connected to the motion picture industry, writing, acting, and I wanted it now!

Ready to Jump

Through the years, I continued listening to *The Secret* on audio-book as my hardcover had fallen into pieces. As a seafarer, changing boats and flying all the time, it wasn't practical to carry books. For me, audiobooks and Kindle tablets are some of the best inventions of recent times.

Listening to Bob Proctor, Dr. Joe Vitale, Abraham Hicks, Deepak Chopra, Ekhart Tolle, and John Assaraf became a daily routine. It was food for thought. Their voices broke paradigms and inspired me to be a better version of myself. The idea came to my mind like a lightning bolt with a fantastic vibration and excitement. I'd risk it all. I'd be bold and venture into the world of entrepreneurship, and I would succeed! I knew I couldn't fail. I would jump to the next stage of being an owner instead of a worker on the time-for-money scheme. Was I ready to jump? Probably! I just needed to figure out where.

That's when I reached out for help and began working the Bob Proctor coaching programs, which is the best in the field as far as I am concerned, in terms of what I was looking for. I wasn't sure yet of what I wanted to do, but I had ideas and I was following a plan I'd set in motion two years earlier. Yet, if I were to reach a goal I already knew how to achieve, doing the same as I'd done before, just for a bigger ticket—to captain a bigger yacht, to get a better house or car, or a higher paycheck at the end of the month—the payoff would somehow feel less than it should. I wanted something that excited me, to keep me alive and kicking, something that would put my vibrations on a constant high. I didn't discard the yachting work immediately, as I still love these yachts. I continued being a good professional while working through the coaching program, seeking the next step.

I knew studying would open my mind, and I would realize where to invest my time and savings to excel on my next venture. And it happened just as expected, but not without a full season of driving a yacht in the Mediterranean before I quit my job. After all, yachting in the warm waters of the Mediterranean is a very pleasurable activity.

Chapter 14

Time for Change

The great benefits of contrast! The fuel to create.

Spending the winter in Dubai was pivotal with regards to my personal life, On the professional side, it was a light yacht with a light usage where I could spend time on the beach reading, at the gym getting fit, watching the best cinema I ever experienced, and studying personal development. Again, I had a top-quality life where money was not an issue. I tend to attract that sort of lifestyle, I guess it's a vibration. Based in Palm Jumeirah surrounded by luxury, the job was a small version of *The Wolf of Wall Street*—partying, drinking, dancing, beautiful women, supercars, and money! Lots of money! I couldn't stop laughing every day, the joy was contagious! I had been warned not to take the job as there was a reputation on the quality of the project, but I wanted to be in Dubai, so I went forward. It is what we make of it, I thought. I took the job and I loved it. Money brings more money even if only in mindset, and for that I was grateful.

We didn't use the yacht often, just a couple of hours on the weekends every other week. No issues on the surface so far. Until one day we had a big spark and flames lit up the electrical panel. This happened repeatedly after repairs, burning through other parts. The yacht was thirty years old and not well taken care of, but we made repairs and carried on, even if a bit scary. Then, like a domino effect, more things burned out, one after the other, and the answer from management was always the same: "Don't worry, we'll fix it in the summer."

Summer was coming and with it higher overall temperatures. It's the desert, right? This coupled with the old boat's poor conditions, created a sense of urgency. It was like cruising in a barrel of gunpowder. With the air conditioning also failing, the entire yacht was a matchbox, although still filled with a great vibe, rose wine, and beautiful women.

I was already looking at setting up a recycling business and moving to Dubai permanently to enjoy the modern Arabian lifestyle.

Nearly Sinking

Eventually, we had a bigger breakdown, this time at night and far away. We came close to sinking. It's a funny story now, looking back!

That day, the sequence of events started with pushing the limits of the engines to high speeds, and that's when new problems developed. We began taking on water faster than we could get it out. I'd been warned that the boat could leak from the shaft of one engine, but I never had any issues at slow speeds. That day, we were going fast to make it to a party a few hours away. We took on a lot of water, but the boss insisted we continue on. Alcohol and cocaine had consumed the boat already, and with ladies and friends onboard, he was loving it.

I suggested we cancel the trip and go safely back to port. He declined and instead we carried on. "It doesn't matter if we sink," he said. "Drive faster. Don't worry, it's my boat." A few minutes later, more issues arose. This time, the water pump broke down so we were literally sinking. I went down to try and repair it, which I did by improvising with another pump from an alternative system. I had a mission: don't be in the news for sinking a yacht in Dubai!

We made it to the party on time, and everyone left to go drinking. I stayed on the yacht repairing the pumping system and removing water. Meanwhile, smoke and a burning smell were coming out of another section of the yacht. An electrical motor had burned out and melted some cables. The entire boat was falling apart. We went for some drinks, and there was great music and beautiful people everywhere. Ibiza style. After a while, we all cooled down a bit and the time had come so we left the party slowly motored the waterways. Shortly after, while running slowly, we heard a loud bang from the stern of the boat—we had lost an engine! I thought the worst, that maybe we'd hit a hidden rock not marked on the charts and now we could run aground, which would be embarrassing and not good with the authorities. The bang was the sound of a gearbox breaking in pieces from sheer old age. After assessing the situation, we carried on with only one engine. We were risking our chance of making it back safely that night, but we finally did. Four hours (and no wine) later, we arrived on the dock and tied her up. We had a laugh, and everyone went to sleep.

A couple of weeks went by and there was no intention for repairs. Instead, there was more excitement about a new plan: we would do a cruise with around eighteen Dubai business billionaires and he would try to sell them the yacht. We'd go out, they'd drink, party, sail around for the day—all just to sell a sinking boat. I laughed at his proposal and replied that I couldn't do it. It went against all my moral values, let alone the safety issues.

That week we'd had another fire threat and now had no air conditioning in the torrid Dubai heat. So, I decided to leave. I still love Dubai!

Once back in Europe I went straight to Malta, another dear and special place, to get a very nice Dutch-built yacht for an American family. We had a fantastic Mediterranean summer, cruising extensively through the Greek and Croatian islands. A fantastic summer of sailing, mingling, eating, swimming, and sunbathing. Although proud of myself and enjoying in general, I was already looking at my growth options and studying through the entire trip. I wanted to be a yacht owner and not a yacht manager anymore. By now I was halfway through the coaching program and it was working wonders, immersed in the Law of Attraction, among other self-development techniques, bringing back the flame of metaphysics and my soul's essence.

Everything was tying up together with what I had used before and with how the Spirit Entity had told me to operate. I was happy and grateful as I felt my time had been worthy of it. I continued studying and applying the same principles I'd used to go from a junkie to a yacht captain. But now, I wanted to go from yacht captain to yacht owner; just a change in perspective, the other end of the same stick!

Inspired by Ms. Rowling

Around this time, I came across an article that said J. K. Rowling had just become the first billionaire author. Wow, what a feature! How much joy did that lady bring to the world to be rewarded like this? Or, what vibration was she on when shifting to the reality where she had a billion-dollar account? How much good service did she do? A lot, making millions of people happy with Mr. Potter's adventures, including me! The great value of teaching and awakening a generation to their magical powers! That was service to the Source for sure! Inspired action and a mission to bring awareness in belief and the joy of magic! That was one of the main messages from my Spirit guide: follow joy, proportionate joy. When you are joy, you bring joy. When you do something from the heart it can only bring love. Our success on earth can be measured by the amount of joy we create for ourselves and for others. That is real success! This triggered me to finish writing my book. An easy, or at least accessible, way to promote and spread the message.

I had an unfinished book based on my near-death experience and Spiritual episode which I had written five years ago to keep a record of the events. Inspired by Rhonda Byrne's success with

The Secret, I'd invested time and love into writing it, and I was very fond of the result. Many topics coincided with the metaphysical side of our existence. I wrote and tried to publish three years earlier in a co-author program with a thought leader, Dr. Joe Vitale. I really believed in the potential of that book as it is a relevant experience. I hoped it could be a bestseller.

At the time I wrote it, I was sailing a lot and living some experiences that I had already committed to, so the writing was somewhat rushed. As a result, I wasn't ready to yet publish my written work. I promised myself I'd finish it later, properly, giving it the time it deserves. After all, it was the depiction of my life. I deserved better than a rushed season. I was on board a magnificent sailing yacht again, living a dream, surrounded by wealth, savoring it, and learning new perspectives from wealthy people. I continued to focus more on seeing and feeling myself as a successful yacht owner.

I did believe that sharing my experience could help millions of people awaken themselves and seek out their best lives. Or at least to have a laugh!

That thought, that vision of myself, was both inspiring and gratifying at the same time. I felt I had a new purpose, one of sharing the light I'd seen, understood, and connected with so well.

Chapter 15

Side Note

Know thyself. The importance of managing adversity.

The title of this chapter minimizes the energy given to what had been my main and only opposition, my nemesis, throughout my whole life, including this period where I felt enlightened. I was one with the love light energy working through me while my nemesis patiently waited for the opportunity to act. I had an eye on it; I could feel its worried and scared presence now that I was one with the Source, but I was not expecting the sneaky ways it moved. The dark side of my life had always been close by, moving simultaneously, waiting for my successes, waiting for my vibrations to rise, or in this case, waiting for my success to show up. My nemesis was always ready to tell me off and put me down, bringing me to lower vibrations, almost like feeding from my sadness and I didn't want to give my power away.

I tried to shut it off with drugs at an early age. That only worked temporarily. Running away geographically helped to some extent, but this was also temporary. The astrologist explained how the position and energy of the planets, moon, and stars affected me. So inevitably, I would have a "great opposition" randomly acting to dampen the light. I knew I had to take an intelligent approach to deal with it. The medium had told me the same thing, that I had a heavy energy dragging me with it, luring me to the darkness. It's part of my existence and I've accepted it. I've welcomed it without fear in order to study it, to live with it, and successfully overcome or ignore it.

Dealing with the Dark Side

After the heart attack, I had plenty of explanations on where and how my opposing forces would come each time I'd thrive and succeed. I'm a thirsty, innovative, and eager person who has always been an activist. That was uncomfortable for many, mostly for those who like to stay put in their comfort zone. I'm a vehicle for light to shine through, and consequently, something would always try to put my light out. Mathematically, there was no way out, but with a way in, I could work around it.

I was a very active and curious child, always interested in the how's and why's of life. I could understand that everything was connected, from the sun, the moon, the weather, and tides, to the birds and bats and dolphins and jellyfish. I could see it all interacting. I was very intrigued by how it all worked. Where are we? What are we here for? What do we really know about our existence and of other planets? When I decided to focus my curiosity, all my energy, into positive and progressive solutions for my life, these solutions were usually radical, sudden, and impactful in various ways. It would create a cause-and-effect domino sequence—sometimes not pleasing the collateral. This process would sometimes trigger disguised and tricky surprises in an attempt to reverse things to what they were before. The paradigm, culture, habits, or traditions. I'd usually try to change these as I'd see a better way. But not everyone wants another way; it took them ages to get things as they are, they don't want to change! However, I couldn't accept the replies, "That's how it's always been done" or "We have to do it this way." Usually, I could easily see another way.

The Supreme Intelligence, the astrologist, and the psychic tarot reader all told me the same thing. They warned me that whenever I tried to do something good, something new or something spectacular, extraordinary, or unusual, I would face a strong and powerful opposition. In other words, each time I'd succeed (and by succeed, I mean being in a high vibration, being extremely happy and in my Super Zen States), I'd have to count with opposing energy.

Basically, the opposition could feel when my vibrations would rise, when I was happy, and sooner or later it would intervene. It couldn't accept me happy. I had to run far from it just to breathe well and carry a smile! That was one of my Spirit Guide's directions: Run, go, and don't go back, never look back! Follow your Joy!

Inevitably, with bright light would come darkness. It's part of the balance. Strong opposing forces would try to stop the progress of this change, to stop me from succeeding, and it has always been like that as far back as I can remember. Now, I would learn how to escape it, taking ownership of my energy.

Looking back at, I could see how and where I failed at the meaningful things I tried to do. Just at the essential part, the decisive point of allowing success, I'd make some erratic move and waste it all away, choosing the dark side. I'd throw away months or years of work in a dark and erratic moment. I would then snap out of it and ask myself, "Why and how did I throw this away?"

This had been a vicious cycle for many years, up until my heart attack. Even during my recovery I felt the dark side hovering over me, making sure I'd stay down, lower in society, wandering in poverty and in need of more, accepting limitation. But now I said, "No. No way. No more darkness. I'll rise. I'll buy my Porsche, I'll have my villa, I'll date beautiful women, I'll earn millions of dollars, I'll have the life of my dreams and be a happy person." The information from the Spirit Entity, the clarity he gave me regarding that topic, was very clear. I could easily "not have it" anymore. I could be no more because it's a choice that I now have, to shine so bright, to be so positive that darkness would leave me alone. Like this, I'd work way around the dark side and negativity by accepting this new belief. Being positive. Gratitude, faith, and meditation, these ideas were my best friends. This way I not only felt true to my nature but also confident in possibilities.

Three weeks before my heart attack, I wanted to die. I had wished for it. I had seen no other way for me to stay alive. The unexpected rejection from my father had literally broken my heart in a new way. It was too much. The sadness that hit my heart had been unbearable. I could understand if in the past I'd been a useless junkie, but I wasn't that person anymore and I hadn't been for the last four years. I was working, I was in university, and I was trying hard to get up and be someone. I had expectations from people, and I learnt not to ever have expectations of people again. Another great lesson learned—don't force anything in life, let alone relationships. Fuck it! The right people will come. Get yourself well, love yourself, be a person you love, and love will show up!

I was ahead of my time, they said, very progressive and innovative, and that would upset the more conservative ones. But I couldn't repress my nature anymore. I'd have to let it shine, use the inner guidance and make the best of it.

The opposition kept coming back, but now I knew how to fight it or go around it, most of the time avoiding it and not taking action whenever the dark side would try one of its moves. What you focus on, you make bigger; so ignoring it was the best option. Now I could only see the light!

Thoughts Are Energy

Thoughts are energy and they will hit us, so we must be strong and protected, surrounding ourselves with those who love us, believe in us, and want to see us succeed. And most of all, we must learn to use the energy of our thoughts to our benefit. Thoughts are energy. Think positive thoughts, constructive of a good personality. Like everyone, sometimes I'd become sidetracked or let my guard down, lose focus, or become distracted with daily minutiae. Managing and using my thoughts was a full-time job, and it paid great benefits. And sometimes it's great to be sidetracked, to miss a class and take a walk in the park, just because it feels good! Enjoy those glorious spontaneous moments.

Intuition! We have to follow intuition, listening to the voice within! I say all this just to clarify that this decade and a half of bliss and opulence sailing the globe wasn't always an easy ride. There were hard and difficult moments, but they were much fewer in number than the good moments. Maybe once a year an issue would arise, and that's not a bad average. As I lived and hung out with billionaires, movie stars, racing and sports personalities, enjoying the amazing places and perks of this life, attacks would come from different angles attempting to bring me back to my old life. This both saddened and scared me because not only could I clearly see who was willing to get me back to my old self, but I could see the way they were trying to do it. It was an eye-opener on human behavior! This area is where I've employed all the teachings from my Mentor up in the clouds. He told me this would happen. He told me to watch out for specific people who would keep seeing me in my old behaviors, and I did keep a watch. This was my life we were talking about now.

My Mentor also told me how to deal with people like that with class, love, and respect, and to do so anonymously and honestly. We don't need to do much; just send love back to all who don't love us, as they're the ones who need it the most. No need for revenge, no need to fight or hurt anyone. Defend yourself, yes, but with love or by simply ignoring it. And so I did, and it worked. "Go and don't ever look back," he told me. "Cut and carry on, evolve, and go have fun. Be fantastic where you're appreciated. Excel, thrive, and be who you want to be. Do and have anything you want. This is how it is. You deserve it. It's yours. I'm allowing it for you, you're worthy, so show me your best self! The best version of you awaits. It's here! Show me you have the courage to take it." And I did. I know it sounds like a lot of words, but the intensity of the information block translated is what it is! We are beautiful, powerful, energetic beings.

It was simple, but not easy. Thankfully, I got it right. I built my strengths and moved on. And I'm still going!

Chapter 16

Action and Conclusion

can't say it enough—life is the true gift, and it's purpose is to be enjoyed!

My journey of becoming my best self isn't even close to being over, and so far, has taken me a long way. It's a process of becoming! I went from being a beggar to an independent world traveler. I could now book flights anytime to visit family, friends, or my girlfriend, and I could gift them lavishly. I paid them back from previous loans and mended most bridges. This was unthinkable just five years earlier. I did it only after I chose to, decided to, and *believed I deserved it*. I gifted loved ones with trips, and most of all, I satisfied the wishes and needs of my closest ones with love and pleasure. My life got better, and so did the lives of those around me.

Improving myself was the door to improving my life experience. The unconditional love and gratitude of being alive on earth allowed Spirit to come in and to express itself through me. I had to love myself first, be my own best friend, study life and the world we live in, imagine a favorite world for me and bring it to my experience. Life showed me who and where I was by giving it back!

My group of friends changed, my places of work changed, and even my distractions changed. I met good, giving people who showed me how they lived, applying progressive and practical ideas and supporting one another. New job offers kept coming in from interesting places I had never heard of. I started receiving more money, traveling more, getting into the exclusive places of the globe, and being treated like a guest since I've accepted that I was a guest in this beautiful planet. I was in charge now. I knew I had made a decision for living in the abundance of love and light.

The Gift of Life

I was enjoying the gift of life and celebrating the joy of being alive, that was easy, so life gave back many gifts for me to enjoy! With appreciation and gratitude for what I had, I received a million times more.

How did I manifest all of this? By believing in it. By choosing the outcome of happiness instead of drama. By observing happiness instead of conflict! Focusing on my chosen desires and enjoying them! When I realized I was alive again, I got so fueled up with enthusiasm and gratitude that I couldn't stop the joy in me. My permanent state of joy for this setting, a planet for us to expand, led do daily lucid dreaming of everything I always wanted to try. I knew that now I could get them, or at least experience them just by wanting to. Then, I realized nothing was stopping me except my own focus. My choice! Nothing was holding me back except for myself. So here I am, alive, and full of excitement with desires to be fulfilled. My mind races with dreams. When deciding a career, I was buying yacht magazines, making vision boards with the favorite yachts I wanted to sail, the car I wanted, and the money I wanted to have. Even if I believe money is a direct manifestation of a state of being, I was tuning in to it. Reading biographies of successful people. I had the desire to experience this lifestyle, the $100 million lifestyle, accepting it! I did what I had to do to receive it, and when the window of opportunity came, I took it. I asked for it, I called it in, I acknowledged it, I owned it, I put the action in and allowed myself to experience it! It was mine. I built it, and it was for me!

The point here is to understand the process of making yourself believe in a dream reality, creating it, and taking it; literally building it with your imagination. Believing I could have it; believing it's okay for me to desire it, and believing YES, I want it, I can have it! Changing the beliefs was the main job! It's the mindset, the decision to create the circumstance and take it when it shows up at your door! I closed my ears to negativity, I listened to my heart's desire, I believed it was mine, and I went for it! And so can you—anything that you desire!

If you get nothing else from this book, please understand this: I went from a self-destructive, dark, and nasty rock bottom of drug addiction, prison, depression, suicidal tendencies, and all the other consequences of that state of mind to a fantastic, happy, joyous, loving, exciting, eccentric, person with fulfilled vibration. Consequently, I received a blissful lifestyle of love, kindness, acceptance, caring, and living in a world of ease, pleasure, joy, luxury and top quality. I did it! I did it by changing focus! And if I did it, so can you.

It starts with a desire to change. A deep, meaningful desire to change, believe in a desire to live well and happy. Fear hovered for months, playing its cards; the fear and paradigm cards were on the table. And do you know what? I knew the results of doing nothing about it. I knew the results of wishing for something and not taking any action in order to get it. So this time, I changed who I was and paid no attention to fear. I focused on my dreams, on love, and the happiness of actually living the dreams as a choice. And I listened to my intuition. The decision to go be it, and let it happen! It has to be an inside job, a click, a decision to go for it regardless of opinions. Just talk to yourself about your dreams, make a plan, write it and rewrite it as you go; take action, make it happen, and enjoy! Allow yourself a fantastic life!

Look inside, focus on the purity of the love energy you are made of. Recognize who you are and choose. I keep writing. I keep dreaming and planning. I keep adding new realities, and I keep living them. Life is a fantastic experience!

Lots of love,
George Adatsi

For more information, please visit:
www.SalMelloBreyner.com

About the Author

Born in 1977 and raised with a large family in Portugal's beautiful countryside. Surrounded by nature, he soon realized his tremendous desire for knowledge and experiencing the world we live in. After an unsuccessful attempt to study art in university, George embraced a life at sea. Traveling the world's continents, sailing its oceans and beautiful coasts became a passion, along with the metaphysical, cosmological, and spiritual aspects of our existence. These are the main topics in his book. It is an experience on the physical planet reflecting inward to explore the soul and outward to explore the cosmic consciousness or our origins.

George's rollercoaster of a life is depicted this book. He's currently working on second volume, and plans for his story to reach the big screen to raise awareness of our full potential as Spiritual Beings living in a physical body.

HEARTS to be HEARD

Giving a Voice to Creativity!

With every donation, a voice will be given to
the creativity that lies within the hearts of
our children living with diverse challenges.

By making this difference, children that may
not have been given the opportunity to have their
Heart Heard will have the freedom to create
beautiful works of art and musical creations.

Donate by visiting
HeartstobeHeard.com

We thank you.